AFRICAN WRITERS SERIES

Founding editor · Chinua Achebe

AFRICAN WRITERS SERIES

125

The Thirteenth Sun

The Thirteenth Sun

DANIACHEW WORKU

HEINEMANN
London · Ibadan · Nairobi

Heinemann Educational Books Ltd
48 Charles Street, London W1X 8AH
P.M.B. 5205, Ibadan · P.O. Box 45314, Nairobi
EDINBURGH MELBOURNE TORONTO AUCKLAND
SINGAPORE HONG KONG KUALA LUMPUR NEW DELHI

ISBN 0 435 90125 7

PR
9408
E83

Printed in Great Britain by
Cox & Wyman Ltd, London, Fakenham and Reading

to TEWODROS GEBRE-AMLAK

Make the flame flow and the fountain smoke
On an adamant floor a handful of sand I'll sow
Fragile pebbles to harvest come the season of dearth.
There is not much else to do
Don't you see, the castle's heroic gun-rest
Is as from today a favourite decaying spot.
Crystal images to skin ourselves on, O Lord.

SOLOMON DERESSA

Part One

1 *Goytom*

Along the main street leading to the hills of the little township, Bishoftu, thirty miles south of Addis Ababa, bill-boards are planted at every conspicuous curve, advertising various commodities, most of them products of the tobacco monopoly. They carry names of beautiful animals, some of them rare and on the verge of becoming extinct, names of queens and famous places from the grandeur of Ethiopia's past, heralding them, it seems, to the new era of civilization. 'Smoke Gureza', 'Smoke Nyala', 'Smoke Walya', 'Smoke Elleni', 'Smoke Axum – Filter American Blend', 'Smoke Marathon – Little Cigars', and 'Fly Ethiopian Airlines – Thirteen Months of Sunshine', they announce.

To the right and to the left, electric and telephone poles criss-cross the sheltering trees and hedges studding the sides of the hills: 'the devil's business' the villagers are pleased to call them. Lamenting their inaccessibility, longing to get rid of them. And haven't they succeeded? With the help of nature, of course. More often than not, thunderstorms and lightning shatter these poles to pieces. White ants eat them from beneath the ground. Monkeys swinging on the wires loosen the ties on the top. And gales of wind from the side give a helping hand to down them on every storm-swept slope. And the natives? Sure enough, they are always ready to give a finishing touch to a 'God-sent' mishap. They tear up the ties to clear up the way, cautiously pull out the steel rails and pull down the telegraph wires. No – not for mischief's sake, as some people say, but from goodwill and pure co-operative zeal. The rails to beat into plough-shares, sickles, spears and knives. And the wire for bracelets and anklets with which to adorn their females.

The ladies' man of his time, carried by his four servants on a litter, Fitawrary Woldu, led the way. His daughter-to-be holding a bundle of wax tapers wrapped in red cloth in her left arm and brandishing a stick which she had picked on the way in her right hand (once in a while, beating off the grass and the leaves) came next. And I, carrying Fitawrary's ·38 calibre pistol with a shoulder holster, brought up the rear. Seven of us, leaving the main street to

2

Bishoftu, turned right and entered on an inconspicuous, muddy track. And we walked up dragging our legs along the never-ending ascents and descents, windings and detours, towards the mountain top, Zekwala, where there is the holy water of Abbo known for its miraculous healing powers.

'You've more faith in white doctors, haven't you, Goytom?' the Fitawrary spoke. 'You grovel at their feet. They're your Gods. Why, it was even your wish to see me die under their butcher's knife.'

Well, what could I have said to that? I simply listened to him.

'I'd rather go to some priest who heals through whispered spells and gobbets of spit than to a doctor.'

'You know what you want, don't you? And you go for it,' I said, not wanting to aggravate him by my silence.

'I most certainly do!'

Dodging the rugged chasms and escarpments, gashed by torrential downpours, we walked and walked upwards, the earth falling away at our feet – tiny dried-up watercourses, ranges of hills, cliffs, jutting spurs of rock, buttresses, scattered groups of juniper and other conifers, and many large woods of *koso* trees, with their red-gnarled stems, bright green leaves and pinkish and bluish-mauve masses of flowers, used as an antidote for tapeworm – falling away and at every ascent disappearing into a dreamy blue haze. And yet, not falling away at all, as if the distance to the top had started to increase, the mountain receding as we struggled to approach it. And our hearts, aching – O Lord, have mercy upon us! Then the half-uttered, half-mumbled order, 'Let us rest a little, boys.' How quick we were at hearing the order and responding to it. The servants immediately stopped and brought him slowly down from their shoulders at the foot of some shady tree – and then we tried to catch our breath.

'Have you heard about the Anti-Christ who will rise before the Day of Judgement? The time has come, the eighth millennium, when he will rend his chain and gain possession of the world. Who knows, perhaps, you and your kind are here to prepare the way for him.'

'Where do they say he is chained?'

'Don't tell me you would go to rescue him if you knew.'

'I guess he is not coming in sandals made of bast-fibres and in undressed sheepskin as in the olden days.'

3

'Why, he'll come in the greatest of splendour – with the sun on his right hand and the moon in his left.' His face became yellowish-brown. His eyes closed in some kind of deep meditation. A rattling sound escaped from his throat. His breathing became a light whistling snore. And it seemed a spasm ran through his body. Then he opened his eyes. Looked around haggardly once or twice. Made the sign of the cross in silence. Closed his eyes again. And lay still.

I could imagine him though, harping on his favourite theme – the gist of all his talk.

How he goes on! As he keeps saying: 'If anything happens to me, you're to take me to Debre-Libanos for my final resting place. It's all put in black and white in my will, you know.'

'You mean when you die?' I say.

'Yes, when I die!' he says.

'We've talked about that a lot of times before, haven't we?' I say.

'Yes, we have. And I'm reminding you again and again in case . . .'

'In case I forget?' I say.

'In case you're entertaining the idea of putting me at another place,' he says.

'My right of inheritance will immediately be annulled?' I say.

'And half of my property shall go to those who uphold the cause of church building throughout Ethiopia,' he says, 'and the other half to all the people who shall take part in the prayer for my salvation.'

'I wouldn't have minded if it were for the building of schools,' I say.

'You know well enough that I don't go for that kind of rubbish,' he says.

Looking down on the sides of the hills, you saw some cultivation, here and there: *teff*, corn, wheat, and other grains of mild climate, chilli, pumpkin, potato and tomato; and looking up, you saw groves of wild olive trees, *wanza*, various sycamore, figs, *woiba*, and the wild, climbing pink pea covering the forest trees to the very topmost branches, and hanging down in festoons of bloom. You saw ferns, such as stag-horn, grasping the tree-trunks, jessamine, and different sorts of convolvulus, and still farther up various cacti, aloes, and euphorbias which appeared distorted, half buried as they were, in low clouds clinging to the mountain top. And you thought you heard Fitawrary's voice cracking again. And you were right most of the time. Something like, 'The fact that we may not make it to the church before mass is certainly a punishment inflicted by God upon us for the sinful life we have lived', he would say. And you knew that it was time to start on your journey – up and up and up – the flanks of the hills and the clefts, full of grey mist, growing narrower and narrower as they ascended towards the clouds. And the mists growing thicker and thicker until the whole mountain was covered with gloom. Up and up and up as if you were destined to reach the firmament. Your soul was filled with restlessness. Your heart stirred in disquietude. And fired as with intoxication and incomprehensible thoughts, you continued walking until you had a sinking feeling that came from a state of extreme exhaustion where legs no longer seemed to swing from the hips, but from the ankles in a kind of loose shuffle – the next to the last stage of stumbling and weaving. But just in the nick of time, as if in a dream, you always heard the heavenly rattling sound of a voice, 'Let us rest a little, boys.' And you rested. You rested and tried to open your eyes and ears – the eyes and ears that had been numbed by the extreme fatigue. You tried hard to really hear what you hear and to really see what you see.

Drawn and haggard faces peeped out from every bush, looking with their hollow eyes and sunken, corpse-like cheeks. The area resounded with cringing, whining voices, 'In the name of Saint Abbo. . . . In the name of the Virgin Mary. . . . May Saint Abbo heal your sick. . . . May the Immaculate Mary be by the sick man's side and give him strength to stand his pain. . . . May the Heavenly Father be your consolation in your sorrow and affliction. . . .' A sort of dusty, nondescript colour of old decaying wood, the faces – they prayed in vain for alms from the passers-by. Typical of sacred places.

'What makes you sure the Antichrist will not ravage the sanctified grounds of Debre-Libanos?' I asked aloud at long last.

'It's written . . . ,' he started.

'Oh, in the Life of Saint Tekle-Haymanot?'

'Yes!'

'So it's either carry your body there or lose the inheritance.'

'And don't forget that you do the carrying on a litter as of old. It is not my wish to be nailed down in a box, dumped in some kind of vehicle and hurried to my grave.'

'You want it to be slow and dignified with all the seven stops, psalm readings and lamentations.'

'That's right.'

'I pray to God, and I mean it with all my heart, that you recover and live long enough not to desire anything of the kind – not to desire anything at all.'

'It's high time you realized that and prayed fervently.'

On some of the hills, you saw nestling some solitary half-rotten human shelters (leaning walls and dilapidated roofs) with their cabbage gardens – brown cabbage, white cabbage, red cabbage, savoy cabbage – around them. And from their hole-like doors, you saw issue out their inhabitants – stained, it seemed, by the sun, by the dust, and by the rains, and all of them reminding you, again, of the dusty colour of old decaying wood.

A little way off, on a mound, near a tree, a stout woman was resting, a small bundle under her head, obviously exhausted from walking. Her thick lips were parted in an ungainly smile – one of the many unsuccessful mothers, perhaps with hopes, delusions, frustration and the desire to be something. And I was returning to my group when I saw a crazy-looking person come by and kick at her. He seemed to dislike her pose and was determined to wake her. I seized him by the collar, and shook him a little. The woman groaned and went on with her sleep – Holy Mother of God!

And then, among the pilgrims, the beggars, horrible to look at in the rags which covered their bodies, with sticks in their hands, and large sacks on their backs – some suffering from leprosy, some from consumption, some from crippling rheumatism, and some from venereal and skin diseases. How they stared at you, surly and without restraint – now coughing and now hooting and now gesticulating and vociferating. You wished you could sink into the ground. But then, a maiden in clean dress would pass by, an elderly gentle-

6

man would unbuckle his pistol in order to recline in comfort under one of the shady trees. You plucked up courage and somehow wished to live despite everything. You would open your coat, blow out your chest as hard as you could, and start wending your way to the church.

Some of the young pilgrims walked faster than you, sweating and drawing their thumbs across their faces and flicking the sweat away. Some, like Woynitu, lagged behind. Beautiful Woynitu! Struggling to put one foot after another. Struggling! And the heat stifling us all like three thousand years. A lean old jackal shedding her coat appeared from some bush, sniffing, perhaps, for a decomposing body. You ignored her and went on walking – up and up and up until you were almost overcome with fatigue. Your whole body seemed to be under a weight, as if overborne with a quintal of *teff*, and your eyes started to hurt with a multitude of fast-whirling, blinding dots; your legs refused to obey you; hawks circled in the air above you and called to one another, fluttering against one another's wings, some rising upward on the wind, others suddenly descending as if wanting to alight on you. . . . 'No, not here, we'll rest a little way up!' Fitawrary would speak as if from some bottomless pit. And you would go on walking upwards, the bell droning somewhere high and distant, and the church seeming still very far away. You struggled panting and puckering up your eyes; and what did you see – fog, mist, bush, a cross-road and a naked tree by the side. And then, of course, 'I guess we can rest here a little, boys', the God-sent commandment.

You snatched your coat from your shoulders, dug into the pocket for a cigarette (despite Fitawrary's detestation of it), lit it, spat through your teeth like a man, gave a nonchalant nod to yourself and sat down fanning your face with a branch of a *besanna* tree.

Thrushes, finches, sunbirds and some busybodies chattered everywhere in the low thorn trees. Goliath herons rose, flapped their wings lazily to a great altitude and then sailing and circling, their long necks outstretched, uttered wild piercing cries. An ass, disturbed in his slumber, brayed in a loud and injured tone, then after a few protests ungraciously stopped again. The solemn sound of a bell came at intervals from the church – the metallic sound wafted from the top of the mountain, melted into the hearts of the hills and slowly died away. 'We must try to reach the church before the mass is over.' Fitawrary would start again and up you were on your way.

But the leg, you know, refused to function; it was asleep, and you had no chance now to stop and wake it. Fortunately, however, you saw Woynitu putting all the energy she had left into the walk and catching up with you. Or a woman in a white dress, a piquant little lady in a state of amorous fatigue came by, riding on a mule and followed by a girl and a bunch of retainers. And she looked at you with a sort of quiet look – and then, the lift of the shoulders, the twitch of her legs as she passed you by. You forgot your leg, and you walked until gradually you noticed that all of you were walking strangely and a little side-ways. One of you started to spin some nonsensical yarn to forget his fatigue! 'The soles of my bare feet are burning . . . we shall have to stop and rest . . . I think a thorn has pricked my foot . . . the thorn is getting deeper and deeper . . . I feel pain all over my leg . . .' An ordinary servant as he was, nobody cared to listen to him. I didn't, for instance. I felt angry about something else – the cantering mule of the lady. He was carrying her away. And then another rider came by and the lady gave way to him as they approached a mud puddle. He splashed her, nevertheless, splattering her legs, and though she tried to save herself, she managed only to spread the mud all the more on her dress. She started riding faster and faster. So you wouldn't have a chance to feast your eyes upon her to the full. Black shreds of thought drove through your mind like clouds after a storm. Your throat was blocked. You wanted a drink of *tella* so badly. And the only other thing which would assuage that yearning of yours. . . Well, you didn't know at the time – perhaps coffee, no – you didn't know. And then something began to rumble and gurgle in the sick man's chest. He began to twitch and roll convulsively. You began to think, listening to him, that he must be a wizard, and master of these remote cliffs, ranges of hills, buttresses and the table mountain – that he it was who originally planted the church in this killing ruggedness, and wantonly dotted the hills with those rotten hovels – that it was he who had poisoned men's brains with complacency – that it was he who devoured their hearts with stagnancy and decadence – that it was he who was responsible for this deadly existence. Yes, it came to you that it must be he who was begging all along the road; he who was hovering like a crow, or he who appeared at the cross-roads as a lean old jackal; he who splashed the mud on that woman, he . . . he . . . he. . . . You swung from the ankles in a kind of loose shuffle, stumbling and weaving . . . you dreamed you had arrived at your destination – Chiqwala or as it is now called Zekwala.

The Awash river, as if slowly eroding you, encircled the mountain to the east. And far away on the flat land, along the way to Bishoftu, a train to Djibouti rumbled on, leaving in its wake torn ribbons of grey smoke that added to the already heavy accumulation of cloud.

2 *Woynitu*

The afternoon sky was blazing hot. The bright glare hurt the pilgrims' eyes. Goytom had gone down one of the hills to rent a hovel. And Woynitu was standing by her father, until she started to walk away to one of the near-by bushes without seeming to be aware of what she was doing, no doubt trying unconsciously to escape the old man's complaint.

'So the church service is already over, after all,' he was saying, 'you didn't bother to arrive here on time, did you? Resting as you did at every bend and curve—'

All the way up the mountain, nothing much had happened which she couldn't describe to herself in thoughts or words. She had seen peasants standing by the thorn fences of their dilapidated huts with their home-spun cotton clothes covering even their proud noses. She had watched the Galla girls, with their garments wrapped round the waist and hanging down to the feet, and with their hair fancifully dressed and plastered with butter. She had enjoyed looking at the ground starred with salivat, primulas, and geraniums and gladioli. She had even taken a drink of water from a spring, drinking from a hollowed trunk laid in it like a pipe – very refreshing, that cool shady spot. And yet she had felt unhappy all the way up. Some kind of puzzle had taken root in her. It worried her in the back of her mind and left her uneasy.

Leaning on one of the trees in the bush, she started busying herself with imaginary adventures. She is working for the Ethiopian Air Lines as a hostess. Flying across Africa and Europe. At one time the plane has an accident. She dives out of the aeroplane without thought of peril and swims through the air. And then Goytom parachutes to save her.

She is a secretary way off in one of her imaginary lands. She quarrels with her boss and leaves the job because the boss tries to make a pass at her. . . . She is leading a new life in her father's house in Addis. And then her mother comes one day and takes her away. Why not? Hadn't she been in the habit of changing her daughter's father any time she felt like it? She might claim her back by saying that Fitawrary is not the real father. Perhaps her idea of a father now is a *Dejazmach*. A step ahead of a *Fitawrary*. Or even a *Ras* – a step ahead of a *Dejazmach*—

A tremor passed through her body. She breathed deeply and tried to compose herself. 'There's something wrong with all my thinking,' she thought.

Sweat started pouring down her face and her eyes burned while she sat at the foot of the tree, looking in the direction of the goat path Goytom had taken.

3 *Goytom*

I tried to approach the scattered huts one after the other and talk to the people who owned them. Hostile towards city-men, none of them was willing to admit lodgers – except one, who agreed to give shelter for two people for the night. Unfortunately, what I needed was a hovel that could accommodate all seven of us and for two nights. After tramping up and down the hills I ran into a man who after a lot of begging, agreed to take us in.

At the gate of his fenced hut, I was met by a boy of about eight sobbing and rubbing his knuckles in his eyes, and by a shaggy dog whose withered body and lowered tail would seem to show that he too was dejected.

My host had to hesitate a great deal and stare into me with his muddy-looking eyes, as though he were expecting something, before he showed me into the hut.

Dilapidated beyond repair, the hut had only two rooms; one big and circular and another small and rectangular. At one corner lay a sick woman. She seemed restless in her sleep. Grunting and snoring, she kept tossing about, with her thin arms and legs sprawling over the floor. For a moment I confused her with the woman that I had met lying by the roadside. At another corner, not far from her, was an earthen dais (*medeb*) with a piece of home-tanned leather over it. It had on it two square blocks of wood about twelve inches long by eight inches broad which I knew were used as pillows.

The wattle sticks and sorghum stalks plastered with mud, from which the hut was constructed, were in many places ripped off and hung in splinters. Everything on the smoke-sodden ceiling stuck down as if the roof were pushing out. On the top of the pole at the centre, covered with soot, hung bundles of millet and corn for sowing. Here and there, bed-bugs raced across the wall. And fleas tapered up through my trousers. And by the door, a small piece of looking-glass hung – a fat spider on it doing her best to cover it with her cobweb.

Well, what could I have done? I had no alternative. The rent agreed, two dollars for two nights, I went back to the church and brought my company into the hut.

Later on, a woman in working clothes with some remnants of faded beauty on her face entered the hut carrying firewood. The host introduced her as his wife and further expounded with pride on her accomplishments – that she had the reputation of knowing what was correct procedure on all occasions, and that she was skilled in exorcising devils, in lamentations, and funeral dances. 'Almost always, the relatives of the people who died in our hut selected her for the lamentations,' he said. She had to inspect her face in the mirror before she gave us her attention.

The face was exceptional in the constant change of expression and the movement of its dark and sharp eyes, which at one moment would withdraw from the door to gaze fixedly and gravely at the sick woman, and at another to scan my face, and particularly that of my father. A fleeting smile would cross her face. Once in a while, she seemed totally oblivious of her surroundings; she bent her head and stayed that way. And when she raised it again, it had another expression. She would bend to help the sick woman, who didn't seem to be aware of the careful attention she was getting and kept on tossing.

The sick woman, in fact, had her own way of comfort – she folded her legs under herself, drew her head into her shoulders, and groped for imaginary clothes with which she tried to wrap herself. Then, after passing through these momentary agitations two or three times, she lapsed slowly back into her original lassitude . . . like a river after an overflow.

Fitawrary, on his part, having placed his ·38 calibre under his pillow, inspected every cranny of the hut – its mud walls and thatched roof with the battalion of bed-bugs, the sick woman, the hostess, and everything else besides, and started talking:

'You know who we are, eh?' beckoning the host with his finger.

'How could I?'

'You must consider yourself lucky having us as your guests.'

'Should I? Oh, here in our parts, you see, we don't open our doors to lodgers . . . and if it were not for my wife making business of it I wouldn't have admitted you.'

'You've heard of the name Fitawrary Woldu, I presume.'

'So many Fitawraries nowadays . . . hard to catch up with their names.'

'The real Fitawraries I'm talking about – those of Menelik not of the Italians.'

'I was too young then to know anything about them.'

'As if the present-day Fitawraries deserve the title!'

'We've two of them in our village; both of them left with title and medallions only.'

'You've got me there, you see, yes – I was talking about the rich Fitawraries, and of the richest of them all – Woldu.'

'I should have known such a name, I think. The problem with me you see, is that I'm behind the news – not going to the village market as often as I should.'

'I haven't made myself clear, it seems. You know, my type is not yet on the market . . . you needn't have bothered to go there.'

'Right you are, I needn't! Everything expensive as it is – *teff*, millet, sorghum . . . '

'Your language smells very much of the soil. Did you not have by any chance a master who could teach you how to talk to your superiors?'

'Oh, lots and lots of them. Why, anybody with money is my master for that matter.'

'I mean men of blood; men who could teach you how to conduct yourself in decent society.'

'How should I know about that? They seem gentlemen enough to me until they get low in the purse. After that they don't even bother to rent my bed.'

'You've a bed for rent, then?'

'Yes, my own bed. I wouldn't mind renting it to a gentleman, sometimes. I'm used to sleeping on the *medeb*. It's good for the health. You might like to rent it perhaps?' Going into the rectangular room, he came out carrying a solid bedstead of wood. Fresh leather thongs were woven over the framework and having tightened in drying, formed a rather hard but agreeable bed. 'You don't have to worry about bed-sores or anything. It's quite comfortable. I might even rent you my own home-tanned leather for next to nothing . . . Should you want it, I mean . . . I shall, of course, give you grass, hay, or straw, free.'

'I'll pay you fifty cents for two days for it.'

'No, no no no! Even ordinary men, merchants and peasants paid fifty cents a day for it.'

'Well, you'll rent it to them then.'

'How could I when you've already occupied all the space in my house.' In his anxiety to have the bed rented, he irritated the bed-bugs in the raw-hide. I longed very much for fresh air and went out.

The change from the stifling air of the hut to the pure wind-swept uplands was great. I decided on second thoughts to go up and visit the church and the lake before the sun sank below the horizon and before the cold set in.

4 *Woynitu*

Roof and walls covered with vegetation and creepers; lichens, ferns, and pumpkins trained up the sides of the house, with their heavy fruit resting on the roof; and cow-chips made into cakes piled around the foot of the walls (why should they use those for cooking when there is lots of firewood around?) – here I am at last sitting by the fence of this hut. And a proud hut at that, with an earthenware crown – the rough, glazed pottery decorating the top of the thatch. And its residents! The hen fussing around, cackling at her brood of downy yellow chicks on a dung heap at one corner; a mean old dog looking suspiciously at me from another corner, growling and trying to show me his ugly teeth; and the lady of the house disdainfully smiling and not deigning to talk to me.

She darts out of the hut and walks away, sloshing the thin mire in the yard, the earthen pot on her back swaying right and left. I guess she is going to the stream to fetch water. And the kid! He is standing by the door, his mouth covered with both hands, one upon the other. Must have been told to shut up. Must be hungry or something. And then seeing me sitting here, he retreats into the hut. And some distance away, two old men sitting on two neighbouring rocks, talking in a friendly manner. They resemble each other. Like those big baboons who were squatting in front of us on our way up here – when we came to them, stalking slowly away like that! I wonder what they would be talking about. Perhaps one has a son and another a daughter. And they are planning to tie them together in marriage. Oh, how refreshing is the smell of the *koso* flowers— And then the girl is expected to drink two or three glasses of bitter *koso* on the eve of the marriage. So the parasites in her stomach get washed out. So that she gets tired and wouldn't be a problem for the bridegroom. How clever they are! After a day's fasting and the *koso* lubricant at the end, she would be as good as dead. And the bridegroom can safely go on performing his duties – without her clawing and scratching him . . .

Strange-looking old men! Perhaps they are trying to settle some family dispute. And one of them coughing as terribly as that! He is perhaps suffering from tuberculosis. Why should he care if he lives or dies, after all. Let him go on coughing his lungs out. Funny-looking people! With their chins covered with small tawny beards, they do not seem to notice their rags and their dirty hands and feet.

And this peasant! Here he comes and stands by the gate looking at them. With his small protruding black eyes which like a jackal's never seem to rest. With his greedy looks, cowardly bearing and his envious air! Just like his dog, he is suspicious looking. I am sure, if I rise and go and try to talk to him, he will drop his tail between his legs and run away. There now! His woman is coming! I wish I could go down to that stream and wash my body. In that small clear rivulet which collects like a bath in a hollow with a rock bottom.

I am feeling unhealthy. With that hooded vulture perching on the earthenware crown of the hut. Perhaps, he is going to come down to the ground in expectation of some offal—I like the marabou, though. So voracious! But individualistic as well. I wish Goytom were a marabou or an ibis, with that rolling note like a lion … And now smoke has started coming out of the huts around. The wives preparing supper for their families … What about the huts catching fire? The thatched roof cracking in the middle, collapsing before my eyes, forming nothing but a huge brazier. Oh, my God. And with my father in it. He would be no more than a glowing cinder – cinder of human flesh … How I hate these flies.

I wonder why they do not place stepping stones in this stinking mire across the yard, so that I can go into the hut without getting dirty. And to imagine that this is where the woman is supposed to be preparing and cleaning the grain for grinding. And where the chickens, lambs and children are supposed to meet and play … What a life!

5 The Volcano

Extinct thousands of years ago, Zekwala's volcano, its lava had retreated step by step, congealing into a series of terraces to form a wide bowl, now filled with a great body of water. It resembled a large mirror, framed all around with rushes, reeds, flags, sedges, and marsh grass, reflecting the blue sky and the fleecy clouds. At one of its edges, the grassy wooded hills reached up to lofty, clayey slopes; revealing, at the very top, amidst a grove of large *koso* and *wanza* trees, the primrose-hued, circular church of Abbo, surmounted by a fanciful cross.

Inside and outside the churchyard and on the terraces of the hills, pilgrims were scattered about. They consisted of dreamers who lived constantly in expectation of some stroke of luck; of idle workmen who, having heard of the fertile region of the South – of free land and wild plantations of coffee – have fallen passive victims to vagrancy; of beggars, who declared themselves to be peaceful, honest citizens whom life's buffetings had compelled to seek prayers; and of pilgrims from the surrounding villages and towns. Some mending their clothing, some killing lice, some munching various types of *injera* collected at the doors of the villagers' huts, some sleeping, and most of them, dirty, grimy, and misshapen, themselves like some unsightly lava freshly disgorged from the inflamed bowels of the earth.

Of all the pilgrims, the most pitiable were perhaps those chronic beggars who had taken upon themselves a disease of the body. Though they suffered by it and complained of it to the passers-by, they nursed it lovingly and used it as a means of obtaining sympathy. Cowed, dull, and furtive of eye, they would be nothing without it. Grovelling close to the entrance of the church and making the sign of the cross now and again, you heard them apologize to you for the least breach of etiquette – as if that was the only thing they had learned through the ages.

They had nothing to fall back on – no kith or kin, not even a celebrated name in their genealogy. Their native land, where every handful of soil had represented to them the dust of their ancestors, and the sweat of their brows, seemed no longer to matter. Confused and mangled for years without number, they had created a habit of living unique to themselves.

On the downs surrounding the lake, the better-looking pilgrims formed various groups. Some were impeccably turned out for the occasion. The girls, especially, looked well off, displaying whole shopsful of Japanese ribbons on their heads, and Ethiopian necklaces, little crosses, and Maria Theresa silver thalers on their necks. But despite them all, the atmosphere left a deadly mark on your person and coarsened it.

At the lake, most of the pilgrims were either drinking or washing their bodies in its holy water. At one point, a maiden who seemed totally to have lost her wits was scouring the earth with her fingers, and scattering soil all over her unearthly face and bloodshot eyes, struggling to free herself from the priest and two other men who were doing their best to pour water on her. At another, a man who could not afford to spoil his trousers by going on foot into the water, was sitting on his horse's back and flailing him mercilessly with a dry branch. His nostrils distended and his ears laid back in terror, the horse kept shuffling along through the deep mud. At times looking as though he were about to fall down, and all the while frantically struggling to escape the beating. At still another point, a lean fellow with sarcastic eyes, and a dark, bony countenance had almost drowned himself trying to swim in the lake. People had gathered around him. And an untidy priest, jostling all and sundry with his shoulders trying to reach the edge, was shouting nearby: 'A cursed fool! The devil in the water must have dragged him to the centre ... the devil must have called him. ... Hell is always the easiest and nearest to hear summons from at such places. ...'

And I wonder if it is not just as easy to hear the summons from Hell in the towns: where everybody and everything is civilized – young men shouting to peddle their various articles; shoe-shine boys running after your feet and almost forcing you to have your shoes shined; a record player blaring at a near-by tea-shop; and the beggars all over the sidewalks crying for alms. 'In the name of Mary, in the name of St George, young man, young lady, don't pass me, don't pass me. ...' And the kids, 'Father, father, I'm hungry. Even a five-cent – a five-cent coin is enough for me.' To how many of these beggars can you give money? And even if you could, there is always the problem of asking a beggar to give you back the change. You will be forced to give him all you have. What else can you do? When God realizes that you have nothing more to give, He should make them stop crying at you. If they haven't driven you mad by then. And those young well-dressed boys! They will approach you and try to speak in English. To show you that they are just as educated as you are. 'Brother, brother! Look, here brother!' one of them will address you. Amazed and a bit frightened, you stop to inquire what is the matter. And he will come to you, 'Look, brother,' he will say, 'I have not eat yesterday, today also. I'm not ask you for much money; just give fifty cent now. . . . !' A civilized beggar who would determine for you how much to give him. You feel like running away from all this. You jump into one of the public houses – a bar, or not liking it, to an adjacent mug-house, or perhaps, you go to the next place, a saloon or a harlot's *tukul*, a photo-shop or a tea-shop — all the same. You wish the earth would open up and swallow you. But the earth never opens. And you go on and on walking wherever the legs take you . . . the same . . . all the same . . . the same . . . kiosk, pedlar, beggar, tart, rubbish-heap, tavern, hotel, blaring record, wench, sweepings, photo-shop, shack, fancy woman, tavern, rubbish, blaring record, sweepings, beggars, photo-shop, cottage, concubine, stubbleleavingsweeds – deads . . . a day of your life over.

The sun had started to sink beyond the horizon. Its heat and glare gave place to the coolness of the evening. The great bowl of water, the hills and the trees assumed a vespertine stillness. The dampness, the smell of rotting grass and mud came more strongly from the bank. The skies got darker and the clouds heavier, and the shadows began to take definite shape both on the land and on the dark green water, some of them assuming the fantastic shapes of strange monsters. Once in a while, you heard the passing shrieks of a water-fowl; or a wild duck, startled by something, would fly out from the lake, clapping the air excitedly with its wings. A cock began to crow somewhere. The mosquitoes buzzed in your ears – and their persistent, shrill cry, resounded in your brain like an endless sorrowful groan.

6 *Woynitu*

What a woman! Littered as it is with rubbish – the walls groaning with gourd and pumpkin utensils and the floor with wickerwork receptacles, earthenware, goat and sheep skins, and the air close and stuffy – she still tries to make a home of it. She doesn't seem to care about herself – with her hair unbound and disarranged. I feel I am already dead looking at her. An invisible cloud of death seems to enshroud everybody and everything in this hut. It may be this life that has intensified the scowl on her beautiful face. The suffering of the agonies of existence. This life with its stultifying lack of variety. I wish it were a dream. And her husband wallowing in a sense of self-satisfaction. And yet she doesn't seem despondent and doesn't seem to complain. She goes on living like a scavenger sifting debris. And perhaps, she will die with a doxology on her lips and she will be buried in sanctified ground near the Abbo Church . . . And how he is looking at me, this peasant. With his deep eyes, black and dreadful like the ooze of a sucking swamp. And look how his gaze is riveted to the column of smoke and fire. And my God! She is going to sleep with him when the time comes. With his body reeking with the odour of smoke and mud. I think he is a madman. Looking at him, I am convinced that he is berserk or something. With his calmly enigmatic gaze . . . And this sick woman who can't recover from the morbid state she is in . . . How I hate this silence. All congealed in their places . . . And then as if she understands my message, she starts talking . . .

'Would you like to have some cabbage?' she asks me, looking over my head. And I refuse the invitation. Then, she looks at me, her face gradually opening to kindness.

'This is the life we lead,' she starts, 'but I had a better way of life,' she continues, 'I passed my youth in privation, wrapped with sorrow – but I had better times.' I can't say a word in answer. Perhaps she wants me to sympathize with her. But the words won't come.

'It's good cabbage soup we have tonight,' says the husband, smiling at me. His way of inviting me. Looking at the pot, as though he is preparing himself to swallow it whole, 'It's good cabbage!' he says. I can hear the small boy swallowing his saliva and heaving a loud sigh and stirring. His father notices it, too. He smiles and the boy feels encouraged.

'I used to sit down on your knees and you used to shake me like a horse,' he says.

'Come and sit down astride my knees,' says the father.

'No! No horse play tonight!' says the mother. The boy remains in his place. Surrounded on all sides by sick people and darkness. A small boy sitting alone in this stillness. A tremendous something seizes me. I go to him and sit beside him. He is frightened of me at first. But slowly, he understands that I mean no harm. He starts touching my dress, my sweater. He even looks me in the face. We become friends. And then I see the father smiling at me – a big broad smile. But his eyes are bleary and his smile is hideous and I do not like it at all. I don't know why. It may have reminded me of other smiles. I go back to my place. I begin to feel cold from the floor made of common earth tightly beaten down. I fold my legs under my dress. Still I can't feel warm. I want very much to be near my brother. I feel sorry for him. He is angry all the time. He wants everything his own way. For two or three days, he stops talking to me if I forget to follow his instructions. Or if I happen to feel unhappy and am weeping. I know he loves me. And he doesn't want other people to look at me. He loves watching me when I bathe and dress. He loves watching me read the books he brings for me. *A Megaton of Love, The Rocket of Love, The Fountain of Love, Love in Secret* – all the books he borrows from the libraries are about love—

'Here's your supper,' says the mother to the little boy, handing him, in the halved pumpkin scooped out as a dish, the cabbage soup with *injera*. And the boy starts eating— I wonder what these people would do without their potatoes, cabbages and pumpkins. And especially the pumpkin: the flesh to eat; the seed to use as medicine for internal parasites; the rind for making bowls to contain food. And the calabashes and gourds which are dried and used for household purposes. One can see that they are not yet devoid of their appreciation for beauty, these people. Their gourds are decorated with beautiful designs . . . Soon after eating, the little boy huddles up in a little ball, hides himself from the cold and from the darkness under a soft heap of rags ... And I start to clothe myself as comfortably as I can with the cotton cloth I wore during the day time, and try to sleep on a piece of goat skin. The husband must be feeling the cold, too. He brings out a tattered army overcoat, his possession from the town, and snuggles into its collar ... Looking at them all, my heart fills with an uneasy dread and from my bottom upwards I feel a tremor which makes my whole body twitch ...

7 *Goytom*

Returning from my escapade, I asked the host to provide me with an armful of straw. And immediately afterwards, I ate my dinner from the *injera* basket we had brought with us, strewed the straw upon the hard-beaten ground, and tried to sleep. It wasn't as bad as I thought it would be, especially because I could have gone to sleep on anything at all after the long and trying journey.

The hostess had already started a fire at one corner of the hut. It was beginning to flicker and tremble when she added to it a handful of dry twigs. It started to smoke, crackled and created a sudden blaze of flame that struck out in all directions. The host, having gormandized his supper, one and a half thick *injera* with cabbage soup, had just risen and gone to his *medeb*. He sat, stretched himself thereon, with hands clasped behind his head, and started to stare at his soot-laden ceiling. Soon after, his wife and child followed suit – and assuming that I had already fallen asleep, the two grown-ups began to whisper to one another in the semi-darkness of the dying fire.

'I'm worried,' started the wife.

'What about?' rejoined the husband.

'You know our landlady will be here tomorrow for the memorial feast of her husband.'

'So she will.'

'What if she knew the Fitawrary?'

'You mean she might forbid us to charge them for their lodging?'

'She might. And if the Fitawrary died, I might be forced to perform the lamentation and the funeral dances free of charge.'

'I think you're right. I should have asked him about it before taking him in.'

'Where did he say he lived, anyway?'

'In Addis, where else?'

'You shouldn't have taken him, then.'

'He may even have a letter from her . . . perhaps he may be hiding it from us until we give him our service.'

'That wouldn't be possible.'

'Why not?'

'Well, you told me yourself that the young man was going from place to place before he came to us.'

'You're right. If they had a letter, they'd have come straight to us.'

'Even then, you should have been sure about them before taking them in . . . the ladies and Fitawraries in Addis, most of them, know each other.'

'It's not late, you know. I can ask him now if you wish.'

'No, not now, you'll do it early in the morning.'

'I'll do it now. And if he knows our landlady, I certainly will kick him out early in the morning.'

'Hadn't you better do it all in the morning?'

'No, I'll do it now.' He rose from his *medeb* and went over to the Fitawrary. The Fitawrary seemed to be in a deep sleep. I would have given anything not to let the man wake him. Once awake, he would never sleep again and I might have to discuss with him the contents of his will for the millionth time.

'Please, please, don't wake him,' I whined, the agony noticeable in my voice. 'My father doesn't know the lady you were talking about.'

'How do you know? You're not the Fitawrary,' he growled.

'I'll pay you the amount for the lodging if you wish . . . yes, I will.'

'All right, pay it.'

'What's the hurry? I'll pay you in the morning.'

'There must be something brewing here. If you aren't paying me now, I'm going to wake him whether you like it or not.'

'All right, all right, I'll pay you now.' I started rummaging in my pockets for the money.

'But I still don't see why you are so frightened of his awakening.'

'That's none of your business. What you want is your money, and you'll have it.'

'None of my business, eh? Why should I take the money from you in the first place? The Fitawrary might pay me more, you see. He has told me that he's a rich man.'

'Here, take all the five dollars.'

He took the five dollars to the fireside, started a small fire, looked at it properly, 'But you owe me only two and you pay me five? There must be something in all this.'

'I'll tell you what it is....'

'All right, tell me.'

'He will not sleep once wakened. And we will all have a sleepless night ... that's why.'

'I don't understand you. If he wakes, my wife will take care of him for an extra dollar or two, you needn't worry about it.'

'But you have already taken your money and that was all you wanted.' He must have been jostling the Fitawrary then, for I heard the Fitawrary groaning and snorting, a sign that he was being wakened. I jumped on the man and tried to stop him. But to no avail. I bounced back and fell on my back. Fitawrary sounded as if he were in a daze.

'I wanted to know if you knew Woyzero ... Woyzero ...' he was saying.

'Ehh ... ehhh ... ,' his hand working under his pillow.

'I wanted to know, you see....'

'What do you want to know? And standing by my side!' Fitawrary goggled – with his pistol pointed at the peasant.

Outside, rain began to pour down upon the dry thatch of the hut shaking the soot on us in lumps. The crickets chirping sounded as if hell had gotten loose. A smell of leather, mouldy grain, and dampness began to issue from the encircling fence. And slowly, the grey, blurred hut drowned in blackness. Rats began their furtive nibbling and scurrying in the wicker granaries. Goats came in from outside and jumped on your clothing and frisked about you. And the incomputable army of bugs and fleas mobilizing under your clothes ... And the Fitawrary ...

8 Goytom

Early in the morning, the bell for early mass began pealing sedately and I rose up. The dawn was almost breaking and the darkness was slowly melting away. Woynitu and the host also rose, and the three of us went up to the church. If I had not been ordered to bring some incense-ash and holy water from the church, I would have preferred to stay in the hut.

So muddy, windy and cold outside. And strange, the boor held Woynitu's hand in his. To imagine that she allowed him to do that! She might have noticed in the evening when I bounced back and fell – might have taken him for a superman. I wouldn't have minded it if I had heard him say something like, 'You will fall on the slippery mud if I don't hold your hand.' Then, I would have said to myself that Woynitu, not knowing what the gesture was intended for, had rejected his holding her at first. But I heard nothing. And she just simply smiled to him with her gold tooth and allowed him to hold her hand in his. I suppose she is sixteen and thinks that she is on her way. Well, why shouldn't she be? After all, I've known her only for about a year.

Many times I have tried. . . . What a way of freezing your heart she has. She would tell you that she is your half-something. Could you imagine it? She has been with us only a year and she would expect me to believe that. . . . There are two boys and another girl of ten at home, who also expect me to take them as my half-something. About six months now since they have come to our house. I guess, in a way, they are lucky, coming as they did from the same mother. Poor kids! They think that they are accepted as sons and daughter when the Fitawrary hasn't even included them in his will. Well, I wouldn't have minded sharing it with them, if only they would stop mouthing that rubbish about their being half-something of mine. No, really, I shouldn't be expected to develop that kind of heart for them in less than a year . . . And could you have imagined it? Woynitu told me that her mother owned a drinking place in Addis – a little less than saying that she is a back-street woman. She expected me to believe that she had lived in Addis all those years and only recently got acknowledged as a daughter.

And my mother . . . what a rich woman she was. She died some five years ago. I guess Fitawrary had married her for her money. And she must have known it. She never trusted him. She had tried to get me another guardian before she died. She thought perhaps Fitawrary would use my money for his other children. And under the circumstances, of course, I had to leave school from the twelfth grade to look after my inheritance. Anyway, I wouldn't mind sharing it with them. I can't help it . . . I love Woynitu's transfixing eyes. I love her smile with that gold tooth shining in her mouth. And I love them all in a languishing way. . . .

And now the boor is holding her hand – looking at her from the corners of his eyes and looking as though he wanted to carry her across on his arms, to swallow her whole, to eat her up like his soup of cabbage and *injera*. Oh, I don't know. I wish the earth would open and swallow him, hands and legs. Or that I were a leopard to tear him down in my turn . . . The pain in my back is still sharp – the pain I got from having tried to stop the boor from awakening Fitawrary. Sure, I will not let him know about it – not for all the gold of Ethiopia. If he knew I was hurt, he would feel elated and might try to show off in front of her. No – I will not let him know . . .

We arrived at the church, at last. Mass had already begun. Thanks to God, Woynitu had also already rescued her hand from the boor's clutch. We entered the church and stood with the other pilgrims in the circular aisle between the outer and the inner walls, where hang various pictures of saints and devils.

At one place on the inner wall Saint Michael, with wings in various hues, and in a costume of red, blue and white, is shown holding up a balance with his left hand and a drawn sword with his right, looking, it seems, from out of his red face to God knows where. The poor wretch of a devil on whom the angel stands seems to stick out from under the ground, opening his wide throat full of bright fire, breathing hotly upon the foot of Michael, and regarding the souls of the unfortunate nearby with his two passionless, pitiless black vents over his forehead.

Standing with his back against the wall, a man was reading to himself from a religious book called *The Revelation of Mary*. Most of us could hear him though: '. . . then He showed me a gigantic and dizzy height – a height that can't be reached from top to bottom in five thousand years. Souls writhing and struggling to climb all over it. I asked my Son whose souls they were. And He told me that they were the souls of those who had sexual relationships with their father's, brother's, or son's wife. Of those who had sexual relationships with women during their monthly periods. Of those who had sexual relationships with Muslims, Gallas, Negroes and black Jews. Of those who had sexual relationships with a horse, a donkey and a camel. Of those who abused the sex act like Sodom and Gomorrah . . . ' And how he was reading each word – with all the humility and respect he could muster. I felt sorry for St Mary who had to witness all that calamity in hell. I wished Mary hadn't gone to visit her Son's kingdom.

And the piquant little lady I had met on my journey up the hills! Supporting herself on a staff flanged with a metal head, and standing at a prominent place near the priests – I felt sorry for her too. Exerting pressure on Abbo or Jesus Christ. Looking solemn and totally absorbed in the ritual.

'And then He showed me another place where I saw an elderly man who was sitting on a bed of fire and was being flogged with fire-whips. And liquid fire pouring on him. And I wept. And I asked Him who that man was. And He told me he was a pope who hadn't followed His commandments and who abused the Sacrament . . . and then another one – a bishop who didn't know that He was One in Three forms. And the devils thrusting fire in his mouth and making him swallow it. . . .' The peasant and the other men and women were oh-ing and ah-ing. Accompanied by the sonorous incantation of Qu'ne poem by the priests:

That's . . . that's
that's to say
Jacob bore
and made
others bear
the teaching
of the Father

the word
Joel
the teaching
of Joel
the father
columncolumn
columnReuben
temple
templetemple
templeEliab
Eliab toiled
built a nation
taught and taught
the word
of Moses
the word
over and over
again
the word
culminating
with the word
Solomon
his cedar
of body
Cedar of Lebanon
Ezek–
Iel
Ezek–
Iel   s a w i t a l l.
Ezekiel s a w i t a l l.

Woynitu is looking at a picture near that of St Michael: a
woman is encircled in the coils of a gigantic serpent – the devil or
the boor or whatever it is – and is vainly striving to free herself from
its fatal embrace. You can see long currents of horrible poison coming forth from the Serpent's mouth – crawling, encircling and pressing the woman down, as if it were crushing her limbs and pouring
itself into her whole body. Dreadfully pale, with hollow cheeks and

deeply sunken, burning eyes, she seems to be in the process of changing into a she-devil.

Woynitu must be thinking about her mother – about the type of torture awaiting her in hell. She may even be thinking about herself – in case she loves me the way I love her. And the peasant oh-ing and ah-ing and standing between her and me. . . . The devils' part is certainly what I most dislike in hell. Standing between you and your God. . . . The scalding fire and the rest of it, I wouldn't have minded. . . . Standing between you and your God. . . . And those series of scenes – showing the various types of torture inflicted on a soul by the devils. In one scene, an angry mob of lean devils with horns and tails and faces as black as coal, haggard eyes and protruding teeth, run after the soul of a fat man with bleeding mouth and tattered garment. In another, this same soul is thrown into the ordeal of scalding water; and choking and spluttering, it is thrown again near by into ice-cold water and gnashing teeth. Taken out of that again, it is thrown into sulphuric fire and subjected to the ordeal of castigation by red-hot iron. With a hand raised to ward off the blows, it struggles convulsively to free itself. But to no avail. Some are wrenching a layer of skin from its body, leaving a raw red wound, some are trampling on it until its entrails start to hang out. And to crown it all, they throw it into the more terrifying section of the fire and leave it to sizzle and shrivel there. A delicate snow-white heap of ash is shown signifying that that is the only remains of it all. Poor old man! No wonder he should want to be taken to Debre-Libanos. And the final scene! Probably to convey the idea that the soul has been forgiven, many of the devils, their hands bound and their mouths gagged, are seen being dragged away by an angel.

Meanwhile, the unchanging chant of the mass wavered to a high, wailing note, soared yet higher towards the cloudy sky, and cooling down gave its place to a refrain which coiled and trickled forth – as if the whole ritual were a grief-laden human life, or as if it were a beautiful song spoilt by a hypocritical singer. You wished to God that everything was over and done with.

I fetched the incense-ash and holy water from the priests, passed them over to Woynitu, and we filed out of the church to the sound of the lugubrious peal of bells.

Looking up, I saw the torn clouds casting their shadows wearily across the sodden earth and silver-dusted herbage. And I felt inspired with a longing to spring to the air, close my eyes, and walk for ever with the seductive sounds of a wasted land crooning in my ears. I thought that the ruggedness of the area had perhaps in it an imperishable force, so powerful that even my puny heart would come to imbibe a little of its fire, and cry to all the universe, 'So what!' and to sing.

To sing the only song that I know:
A miracle
to behold
earth to earth
snow to snow
lightning to lightning
why then subject oneself
to things
a naked man
Is
a naked man
the world, his body
cracked
the sky, his soul
covered with cloud
graveabysmal
Jehovah
universe
unfathomable
will judge both
guilty and innocent
to the measure of
the crop
of the deci-
duous
world
dawn breaks
and evening
closes.

9 Goytom

The morning breeze had started to ripple the leaves and the first sword-shaped beams of day unfolded themselves. A dense sound-wave of voices seemed to pour its creative power upon the hills and marshes from which a reddish vapour as of incense was rising: birds were awakened, and the crowing of cocks, the lowing of cattle and the murmur of human voices slowly filled the air. When I arrived at the hut, since I wasn't in a hurry to go in, I sat down on a block of stone a little way off the enclosure and started to enjoy everything about me – the doves and wild pigeons calling from the foliage of the *koso* trees; cranes, herons, ducks, geese and ibises saluting the coming day in a great clamour – everything as it used to be thousands of years ago.

No wonder Ethiopia is a potential tourist paradise.

Woynitu should have stayed outside and enjoyed the scene for a while. How beautiful she looked walking in front of me and hurrying downwards to the hut. I'd felt like flying away to the heavens with her like the doves and pigeons. And when I think about that plan of hers of being an air hostess – a beautiful girl like her – I feel a heartache. I don't understand what attracts her to that profession. The tourists, perhaps. Or the great conferences of African leaders. Or the commissions – like the Economic Commission for Africa. I don't understand.

She could be an asset, I know. If she went to one of those conferences and simply sat in one of those spacious halls. The cynosure of all eyes – the big men's eyes – she will become. Beautiful Woynitu. She will then help her mother – her country. She will make the big men spend lots and lots of money on her. And especially if she has got the idea of taking some of these Galla girls with their Japanese ribbons, and of washing their hair, changing their clothes and of training them. They will be more attractive that way. And with that Ethiopian hospitality in her.

And then she will introduce me to one of those big men.

She will also take some typing lessons herself. Get employed in

Africa Hall. Beautiful Woynitu – she will make up to one thousand dollars a month, plus the rent for her apartment which her boss will pay from his own pocket.

And then if I wish, I can get employed in one of the departments I will be the confidant of the boss. We will have fun at Woynitu's apartment. We will discuss national and international issues.

No, she wouldn't allow those men to get fresh. She will tell them that the leopard won't allow such things to happen to her. Our income will increase. Our country's revenue will increase. Beautiful Ethiopia. With her beautiful birds and animals. With 'Shooting is prohibited' signs all over the reserve areas. Only once in a while for special guests. No, she will drop the idea of being a hostess. She will simply fly to Europe once in a while. With her beautiful face and Ethiopian hospitality. She will attract many tourists. She will pass the EAL tests if need be – virgin and adept at entertaining guests. Very important to the company. She knows her way about in the towns. She can take the tourists around. And she will have her decent house where she has waiting these beautiful Galla girls. And all those big men of Africa will flock to Ethiopia.

They will raise their hands in consent whenever a meeting is suggested to be held in Addis Ababa. They will raise their hands. With that Ethiopian hospitality. And all those beautiful cars they ride in when they come to visit us. Cars of all varieties. From all over the world. They will ride in those beautiful cars. And the chauffeurs will always be ready to show them some out-of-the-way places. All those big men. They will feel like Gods with their pockets full of money. Because Ethiopia is God's country. Ever since the third century. And Woynitu attracting tourists and all that. She might even arrange some business deal. To export some beautiful girls. Since we have them in abundance here. We will have more revenue for our country. Coffee and hides and girls – the list of our exports will read. And our imports – all kinds of international money.

And all those taverns will be amalgamated to form a company. Sputnik or Rocket or Apollo company it will be called. To make it sound scientific. It would appeal to the civilized tourists. And Woynitu will be rich. Ethiopia will be rich. Ethiopia will be industrialized. She will be a name of international renown. Woynitu and

Company or Apollo and Company or whatever it is. Oh, I don't know. I'm tired of these things. I don't happen to be one of those people who like such industries even on small scales. They will create smog. They will contaminate the water and the air. But then who am I to decide on that. I'm not one of those people on the top. Short or long-range planning is not in my line. It's only that I can't help thinking about it on such a beautiful morning. I feel everything is possible. I feel everything has its purpose in life. I can't help being open-hearted or rather internationally minded. Perhaps, it may be because I see more women and tukuls than homes all over the towns. But then what does it matter as long as they come in handy during conferences. I don't mind really if Woynitu joins Ethiopian Airlines. Beautiful face. Beautiful form. Beautiful national dress.

She won't have to worry if Fitawrary acknowledges her or not. It may be because she is born of a woman who owns a drinking place. He will forget that soon after she becomes wealthy. When she comes back from other parts of Africa or Europe with some beautiful artificial hair for his bald head. Or with some modern false-teeth. She will make him feel young again. She will make him smile. He will start to love her. He will acknowledge her as his daughter. Even as his only daughter. I wish he would disown me then. That would put me on an equal footing with all those admirers of Woynitu. I wouldn't have to take a boss to her apartment. I wouldn't have to let the boss pay for her apartment. . . . How everything seems simple and easy when you rise and investigate it on such a beautiful morning. . . .

The sun had begun to rise higher and higher into the greenish-blue zenith. The crowing of cocks, the lowing of cattle became less and less. Fitawrary came out of the hut carried on his litter by his servants. He was going up to the lake. I guessed they'd had their breakfast without me. They hadn't even cared to look out for me. I went in to have some mouthfuls from the *injera* basket that we had brought with us, and followed them soon after.

Part Two

1 The Sermon
at the Lake

Pilgrims had already gathered by the lakeside. A collection of lovers, gallants, profiteers, state embezzlers who had drunk away their consciences and forgotten the tradition of their fathers, of people of the basest scum, drunkards, thieves, prostitutes, hawkers of every kind of rotten provisions, and ragged, hungry and destitute peasants – these human beings, on each of whose faces were written laziness, slovenliness, weariness, boredom, disenchantment, hate and crime, were here to be cured of their various ailments and to pray that God save them from the current famine, diseases and social problems.

A stout-looking preacher with newly matted hair was standing amongst them trying his best to show the path to salvation:

' . . . there are those among you who live for the body – drinking and eating to satiety . . . ,' he was saying.

A mule, breaking his tether, came along sniffing the fresh air and wandered into the lake, wetting his hoofs and fetlocks. And dipping his muzzle in the water, he began to suck through the lips torn by the iron-bit. Then, leisurely swishing his scanty tail with its half-bald stump, he sniffed at the edge of the lake and, biting off some wisps of grass merely to relax himself, walked to the ridge. The owner, who must have been engrossed in the sermon, didn't seem to notice at first the unattended leisure of his mule. For when he did, he didn't approve of it. He rose up, walked down to him and was about to strike him on his lean leg with the buckle, when he changed his mind, dragged him farther off and seated himself holding him by the bridle.

Fitawrary, placed at a comfortable site under the foot of a shady tree and listening to the sermon, was looking at the mule when he started muttering, 'Who would have suffered more, for example, if that man had hit his mule with the buckle? He or the mule? He was a fool to throw away easy money like that.'

'The mule, I guess,' answered Goytom indifferently.

'No, you're wrong. It's the man who would suffer – the man who would be forced to walk home if anything went wrong with his beast.'

'Maybe.'

'Why in the world that beast changed his mind, I don't understand. He was a fool to throw away easy money like that.'

'Which beast could you be talking about?'

'The one who rented us his hut.'

'It's difficult to predict his type.'

'Refusing to let us to return for the night!'

' . . . There are those among you who having got strength from your bounty, find your outlets with sinful women. Those who have no Christian restraint at all. Such of you once in the mire have no chance of seeing the light. . . .'

'Probably his wife thought that you weren't the type to make business of,' commented Goytom, thinking about the peasant's refusal.

'It wasn't wise of me to refuse to rent their bed, perhaps.'

'Perhaps.'

'He didn't even ask us the rent for the night, did he?'

'Yes, he did, last night.'

'And you gave it to him?'

'I did.'

'The way he awakened me only to ask if I knew that lousy landlady of his!'

'Yes, it was strange.'

'I thought for a minute that the hut was on fire.'

'So did I.'

'He seemed friendly with Woynitu though.'

'Oh, did he? I didn't know.'

'Yes, I saw him smiling to her and wanting to start a conversation with her.'

'I didn't notice.'

'The brute!'

' . . . You may fast and pray, but, it will be in vain as long as your heart is already filled with the venom of your doings. For when you think of God, you think of food and drink; when you think of heaven, you think of money and power; and when you think of happiness, you think of vile music, drinks, and women. Oh, my children, such of you have no heart that prays to God without praying to mammon. . . .'

'How about the wife of the brute, did you like her?'

'Oh, she's great.'

'How so!'

'She knows all the different kinds of roots for almost all diseases.'

'Don't tell me she has administered something for your heart disease.'

'Yes, she has. In fact she has agreed to go to Addis with me to do anything in her power to cure me.'

'May I ask what for instance she did to help you?'

'She gave me some kind of medicine to drink – some compound of root, a hooded-vulture beak, hyena's liver and some other things I don't remember now – all of that mixed with *koso* water.'

'Oh, my God!'

' . . . But there are also others of you who can come out of such bondage if you really try to. If you try hard enough. Yes, my children, if there is the will there is the way. . . .'

'And was that all! She has told me also what the cause of it all was.'

'The devil, I presume.'

'You know I don't like this sneering attitude of yours towards your own tradition.'

'No, I am not sneering . . . I am only trying to guess.'

' . . . Sit not my children at table where there is food in abundance. Be not lovers of drinks. Go not to the house of evil women. My children, for the love of God, eat but little such as a handful of roasted barley and a portion of *injera* and drink not the home-brewed *katikala*, *tella* or *tej* or the foreign imported beverages, but simple, clean, healthy water of our springs. And even if you have to throw a feast now and again, make it with discretion, for the unaccustomed food and drink is an enemy to the stomach of the average Ethiopian. It will make of the stomach a brewing place for intestinal disease, diarrhoea, constipation, vomiting, sleeping sickness, and so many others besides. Why, you yourselves are witness to the bygone days! Were there as many diseases as there are today? Were there so many killings then as there are today? No, my children. I say again and again – eat and drink with discretion, for you eat and drink to God and not to yourselves. And God doesn't wish you to eat and drink to satiety....'

'Yes, she has also told me to make a vow to Abbo to slaughter on his anniversary a bullock, in order to secure his protection and favour. I've already asked her to find for me a white sheep which she said would be dragged three times round me and would be slaughtered at a point where two roads cross each other in the name of the Father, and of the Son, and of the Holy Ghost. She said that the sign of the cross would be marked on my forehead with the blood of the sheep which would be left where it was killed.'

'... Why, your orthodox church has done all it could to clear the way for you. It has fixed for you fasting days so as to give you a chance to abstain from fat and meat. My children! Forget not the fast of Gehad, on Epiphany eve; the fast of Nineveh, for three days; the fast of the Apostles, for forty days; the fast of Lent, for fifty-five days; the fast of the Holy Virgin, for sixteen days, plus the Wednesdays and Fridays, for about one hundred and four days. Why, you will have about fifty-six days in which to eat fat and meat every year. It's of course advisable to seek the advice of your father-confessor to take on yourselves some more fasting days as the need for it arises....'

A woman, bony, and crooked of back, weather-beaten of skin, had been gazing at a small crucifix in her hand with sorrow and moving her lips in confidential conversation with the Saviour.

'When is this prescription of blood of a white sheep to be administered?'

'As soon as she gets the sheep, of course?'

'And I suppose I'm expected to be here for the occasion.'

'Yes, she has chosen you as the right man to slaughter the sheep.'

'But you know very well that I haven't slaughtered an animal in my life.'

'That's no problem – you shall start now.'

'What I mean is that I don't like slaughtering.'

'I do not expect you to like it, only to do it.'

'What if I say no?'

'I hope you know better than to say no to the wish of a dying man.'

'To the wish of a dying man!'

'Now you go ahead and tell one of the servants to dig me a hole by that bush.'

'The *koso* water is doing its job?'

'Yes, and hurry it up.'

'You can't even sit up properly, how ... ?'

'Please!!'

' . . . My children, man is fashioned of divine meat and cemented with holy grease. He doesn't live by bread alone and he doesn't live for work alone. He lives by the word of God and for God alone. Do you know what? Ethiopia is the only country in the world, you may not believe it perhaps, but it's true, the only country in the world that has different patron saints for each of the thirty days of the month. Any man or woman can have the patron saint of his or her liking, and as many as one wishes. Of course, the more saints you have the more time you spend to pay your respects to them and the more bounty they bestow on you. There are some blessed people I know, for instance, who work only for two or three days a month. The rest of the days are allotted to their patron saints and they abstain from any kind of work. I can see that this is perhaps too much for some of you, but at least you can have from ten to fifteen – say – for example, Saint Abbo on the fifth; Jesus Christ on the sixth; the Trinity on the seventh; Michael the Archangel on the twelfth; Kidane Mehret on the sixteenth; Gabriel on the nineteenth; Mary on the twenty-first; St George on the twenty-third; the Saviour of the world on the twenty-seventh. . . . Yes, my children, if you fast, keep patron saints, and follow the commandments of God, everything will be all right with you. . . .'

The devotees lowered their heads, caught their breath, cast their eyes down, and herded sullenly, involuntarily into a group. Some apparently cold after being splashed in the holy water earlier in the morning gazed gloomily at the preacher from pairs of narrow, inflamed eyes. Some were dozing, with their arms embracing their knees, their chins resting upon them, and their red, sleepless eyes gazing lifelessly at the water, their alienated expressions thrown into tragic relief against the cheerfulness of the morning, and the radiance of the heavens.

' . . . If someone robs you, insults you, hits you on the nose, he will only be swelling your account with the Holy Spirit. Rewarding you the right to Heaven for what you have gone through. **But** instead, my friends, if you struggle against what has been ordained of God what would your reward be?'

A man with scanty beard over his lean face, eyes deep-sunken, came from the water. He was wrapped about with wet, clinging underclothing, and as limp as a half-empty sack he deposited himself near one of the groups. The eyes of the preacher scanned him, seemingly engaged in counting the holes and darns in his raiment.

' ... We've a rich land, every sort of natural produce is to be had and the soil is generous and light, you need but to scratch it for it to bear, and for yourselves to reap. ... Why, you must make the best of what you have. Life, as it is, is honey mixed with gall, and it's up to every one of you to enjoy both the honey and the gall, separately and together. Otherwise, you'll die before you have seen a little good accrue to yourselves ...' A certain bombast of pose, and of stern authority, and a noticeable disgust for those on whom his eyes were directed, were clearly visible in the preacher's physiognomy. But the majority of the pilgrims, despite their withered souls, went on listening to whatever was uttered. Listening, as much as to the Christian message of the preacher, to their inner selves, which believed in superstitions, in witchcraft, and in the magical powers of such things as mud or reeds or flags taken from the lake, ash from the burning of incense in the church, and amulets.

' ... And after death, Satan will be there to receive your soul with his thorny fingers and sharp pointed teeth. But on the other hand, if you die, tilling the generous soil, fulfilling the commandments of fasting and of respecting the saints, your soul will fly up to the throne of the Heavenly Spirit, and the angels will extend to your little soul their tender, white, and gracious hands. And your soul will tremble all over, and flutter her gentle wings in gladness. And then, of course, you shall be taken to your Creator for the final judgement. The sinners will stand by the left where hell awaits them open, while the holy ones will stand by God's right, holding palms in their hands. ... And then, He will say to those on His right – ye who have heard my commandments and have lived by them, ye who have given me shelter when I was homeless, ye who have given me food when I was hungry, ye who have given me water when I was thirsty, ye who have given me cloth when I was naked, ye who have visited me when I was sick, and comforted me when I was thrown into caves and jails – for ye all I have prepared a place before the world was created – a place where there is no dirt, no weary quarrelling, no blinding cruel strife of egotism, no tortures of a man arrested in the streets with callous laughter, and beaten by the rough hand of law – a place where everything is pure, joyful, and bright – go live in happiness and total bliss. . . .

'And to those on His left, He will say, ye who have heard my commandments and heeded them not, ye who haven't sheltered me, fed me, clothed me, paid me visits in prison, ye who have totally forgotten me and lived in licentiousness – go to hell to everlasting torture and gnashing of teeth. . . . And they will ask Him, the condemned, O God, where have we met You hungry, thirsty, naked, and without a roof over Your head and refused You, and where were You thrown into jail and we didn't visit You? But He will say to them – go to Satan and his followers whose followers ye have been and whose followers ye shall be to the end of the world. . . .'

A plump and gentle-looking man, with a mouth perpetually half-open, so that the face looked like that of an imbecile, was listening attentively and piously.

'. . . O dreaded God, O beneficent God, O God who sittest on high, and on a golden throne, and under a gilded canopy. . . .' He went on crying out loudly, staring wildly around him, and gesturing with his hands, 'It's for our sins that a crown of thorns was put on Your head, for our sins that You were flogged, for our sins You were crucified . . . but what have we mortals done of it all? O purest Mother of God! O Thou of Spotless Chastity! Forgive these sinners, Thy children . . . reconcile them with Thy Son and help them gain the everlasting place of happiness. . . . Poor mortals as we are, we struggle to advance, to progress, to hold the moon in our hands and the stars as well. We keep pressing forward when we ought to be waiting, to be proving ourselves here on earth. And lo, perdition will arise before us who shall hasten. . . .'

At last the hole by the bush was ready and Fitawrary was led by Woynitu towards it.

And at last, the preacher seemed to have finished his preaching. He lit his wick in honour of the occasion and started to read some words in Ge'ez from a worn-out book. Readings neither he nor his audience comprehended. The wick in his left hand diffused a feeble light in the brightness of the morning, and now and then flickered in the gusts of a desultory breeze, fraught with the odours of marshy water, *koso* flowers and corruption.

The attitude of the men and women was one of infinite patience. And when finally the preacher growled, gesticulated, rolled his eyes about and stopped, a hush fell, and all stood up, confounded and silent, their subdued looks making each barely distinguishable from his fellows. And all seemed to utter in unison, 'It will not be long before he dies and becomes a saint, and we fall down and worship him.'

A priest with a high headgear came forward, and started to breathe the benediction upon the people.

'Pardon O God, sins wilful and of ignorance, sins known and unknown, sins committed through imprudence and evil example, sins committed through forwardness and sloth. . . .'

The sun had moved out of its beautiful phase and started blazing and diffusing warmth, undeterred by the squalor around.

2 *Goytom*

The preacher howling about hell and heaven. Woynitu doing her best to be of some service to her father. Fitawrary hoping to be called to the sacrificial place: to kill the white sheep and regain his health. Hoping to live longer to fight against anything new – modern way of talking, modern dancing, modern dress, modern haircut and tobacco. And hoping to keep on for ever without working with his hands. God's way of putting an end to things. And beautiful Ethiopia full of her several representatives of the cabbage family – brown cabbage, white cabbage, red cabbage, savoy cabbage. And as always stretching her hands in penitence to win from God indulgences for her children in Purgatory. To save them from blazing brimstone and eternal torture.

Waiting for the sacrificial sheep.

Beautiful Ethiopia – with her flat valleys of deep brown or black soil. With her hills sloping gently upwards and covered with barley. And then dropping for some thousand feet and covered with terrace upon terrace of *teff*, wheat, sorghum, and peas. With her delicious sheep who feed on wild thyme and mint. With her fleeced sheep that give the wool from which clothes, *bernos*, and blankets are made. With her endless herds of cattle and droves of brood mares and their foals. With her children parading their bumps from the bugs, lice, and fleas that abound in the hamlets.

Waiting for the sacrificial sheep.

Beautiful Ethiopia: with all men of title – *gerazmach*, *kegnazmach*, *fitawrary*, *dejazmach*, *ras*, generals, ministers, princes and princesses – doing their best to alleviate the suffering in the hamlets. Begging manna from Heaven. Sending DDT. Sending rat poison. Sending insecticides. Sending the police. To alleviate the pain and hardship in the hamlets. And hunger, ignorance, and disease bestowing their bounty all over the country. God's way of putting an end to things.

Waiting for the sacrificial sheep.

Beautiful Ethiopia – with her peaks and cliffs and escarpments piled helter-skelter on the high tablelands and railroads criss-crossing all over them. With donkeys and mules. With patriotism. And with medals, medals, medals – for smoking, for burning, for living, for killing and for dying. And all her children shouting their war cries. Among her giant ranges. Among the isolated mountains of weird and fantastic shapes. Undecorated defenders. And her women grinding grain on the flat stones. On the hard black stones from the mountains. And the paths along the bottom of the gigantic crack of her face leading to her chieftains with their little brown or white or black dogs romping from one stiff attendant to the other with wagging tails. From one retainer with a spear to another with a gun. Wagging their tails. Begging manna from Heaven.

Waiting for the sacrificial sheep.

Beautiful Ethiopia – with her watersheds running along the razor-backed mountains, full of power and electricity. With her rugged and uninviting flat land with the growing grain crops contrasting with the brown fallows and the light yellow or stone-coloured stubble. With transportation facilities all over the farmlands. With donkeys and mules. With war cries of heroes all over the hills. With arms and ammunition. With manna from Heaven. With the war cries and lamentations on bamboo reeds. With her baboons wrestling, tackling, and cuffing in her forests. With her police force in action. With her trees of fig, *koso* and mimosa. With her banks lined with ferns, purple and yellow iris, ranunculus, myrtle bushes and dog roses of many colours. With large clumps of tall maidenhair. Picking raw cotton from the seeds. Spinning and spinning it by drawing from a bobbin to a regular thickness for a thread. Twisting it by rubbing the bobbin on the bare thigh. Letting it spin for a moment – hard-working women. With God's way of putting an end to their nakedness.

Beautiful Ethiopia – with her limes, lemons and other sweet-scented trees. Small rivulets, gentle creeks, and zigzag pathways through the rocks that lead to her chieftains dressed in snowy *shemma*, white tight-fitting trousers and brown cloaks with edges of gold braid. With a brand of a handshake on their backs.

Waiting for the sacrificial sheep.

Beautiful Ethiopia – with the court and church-land defined only by the knowledge of the local people. The land-owners must be shown the marks which bound their properties. While all the chieftains' land may be alienated as the exclusive property of their children. Especially when a title-deed is required for foreign companies to buy land. The people's land, the chieftains' land. Bringing in more and more foreign investments. And the children of the chieftains becoming richer and richer. Wagging their tails to Heaven.

Modern patriots fighting against companies. Fighting for modern medals. With a brand of hand-shake between Ethiopia and America on their backs. God's way of putting an end to things.

Beautiful Ethiopia – with her distorted wild olive trees on far away hills and half buried in smoke and low clouds clinging to the horizon. With her lemons and blackberries. With strawberries and various kinds of stone fruit. With her junipers and euphorbias. With her churches on the top of all. With her hunger and diseases.

Waiting for the sacrificial sheep.

Beautiful Ethiopia – with her vast body of sixty-five per cent arable land. With her gazelle, duiker, klipspringer, kudu, and dik-dik. With her bush-pig, buffalo, oryx, and ibex. With her lion and leopard. With her hunger and diseases that are God's way of putting an end to things – stretching her hands to Heaven. With her thousands of churches and her conjuring men and women. With her cattle and sheep. . . .

O no! I am not going to kill the sheep at the sacrificial place.

3 *Woynitu*

These men, these men – Fitawrary, the preacher, the peasant – why are they all the same? What has taken from them their sense of humanity? True, I'd never known my father until I was fifteen and that because I failed my sixth-grade examination twice and refused to fall in my mother's line. And my mother keeping a tavern! Perhaps she finds it easier to live that way. After all, what else is there that she can do? Disgusting as it is, this life of hers, yet she lives by it. Really disgusting – dealing as she does with all sorts of degenerates. She is kind-hearted, my mother, but uneducated. She never cared, for example, about my taking liquor when a customer came along and bought me a drink, taking me to be of the same calling as my mother. She thought it helped to add to our little income. She even sometimes left me with strangers and enumerated for me their qualities in advance – mostly about their being rich and men of status and influence. It occurs to me now that she didn't even seem to notice when pimps tried to approach me. No – I'm by no means blaming her. She could not have helped it, hemmed in as she was by house rent, municipal licence tax, and the food and clothing she had to provide for both of us. Besides, she'd had to pay for my schooling. And the ever-increasing industry of taverns and night clubs she had to compete with! It's simply staggering.

So, what could she have done? She would have avoided it if there was a chance. But as it was there wasn't. And what did she expect from me? A little help – that was all. Though her way wasn't my idea of it. Sure enough, I wanted to support her – but in a respectable way – by getting a job somewhere, as a clerk, or even as a maid, why not, in one of the restaurants. It didn't work however. There also were the vultures, including the proprietors themselves.

44

What a year I passed with her after I had left school. Her pressure on me growing day by day until it looked as though she was determined not to support me any longer. And one day that incident which put an end to my ties with her. I can still see and hear everything that took place that evening as if it were today.

Three men were at our house drinking. They treated my mother to drinks until she was drunk. And she had to leave me in charge of everything and go to bed. In a way, I didn't fail her and did everything in my power to entertain the guests. And they seemed very much pleased. Pleased to the extent of calling to our *injera*-baker leaving for home after the day's work, and buying her several drinks. After which all of them left. . . . And then, some time later, the return of our *injera*-baker. I thought at the time that she had forgotten something and come back to take it. But no! She was back for something else. She came towards me as if she had a secret to confide in me. I wasn't at all suspicious. And so she sat and started to talk, shy-like:

'I hear that your mother has again taken a drop too much, hasn't she? God knows why she does it.'

And I say, 'I thought you had come back to tell me something.'

And she says, 'Yes, my dear – yes, but you see, I'm really in a fix. I don't know how to really put it.'

And then I say to her, 'Look, don't be all that disturbed. Just say it out and be over with it.'

'Please, first of all, don't ever think that I will get anything out of it.'

'Out of what?'

'I'll get nothing out of it. But you see, this youth, this beauty of yours, it's these things that make me want to do something for you.'

'O yes?' I say.

'Why, you could just go out and see for yourself. Even the light alone that comes out of your eyes could have conquered the world for you,' she goes on.

'O, it could, couldn't it?' I say.

'And if you really come to know this gentleman – handsome, rich. . . .'

45

'Sometimes, I'm surprised at you,' I say.

'If I don't get the chance, he says . . . ,' she continues.

'He will kill me perhaps,' I add for her.

'Well, you know, he might send his servants . . . I'm sure he will. He takes much pride in his wealth. . . . Please, my dear, don't be stubborn,' she says.

'I don't have the heart for that kind of thing,' I tell her.

'Well, you don't have to do anything, if you don't want to. Only talk to him, that's all I ask,' she says.

'I don't think you understand me,' I say.

'Let me assure you about that, you see, the gentleman is ready to do anything for you. He says he will build you a house of your own, buy you a car and even deposit for you a lump sum in any bank you wish. . . .' she goes on.

'Then let others profit by it,' I say.

'You don't mean you are going to refuse such an offer?'

'I'm not an article for which he can build a house and deposit, you see.'

'Oh, you want to be decently married, don't you?'

'Yes, if I get my kind.'

'So, you have come at last to your senses, haven't you? Now, I see the God of your fathers spreading his divine light on you,' she says. 'I tell you, I'll try to find some elderly people and have them draw up a contract for you as his wife. No problem about that,' she says.

'You mean he wants marriage?' I ask.

'In a way, yes,' she says, 'but, you see, he may not live with you in the same house. He has a wife and children, and . . .'

'So, it all boils down to this, doesn't it?'

'I don't think there's anything wrong with it, is there?'

'Please, leave me alone,' I say.

And then she says, 'If you refuse when you are begged, you know, sooner or later, it's likely that you will yourself come begging. . . .' It was so involuntary a movement, I really didn't know how it happened until I struck her on the face.

She left the house cursing and vituperating, and I left in the early morning, praying and hoping that perhaps there would be a chance at my father's – the father I had never had a chance of knowing.

And here I am at last going back and forth to support him to sit up by the bush.

4 Fitawrary
Woldu

The point is that I cannot go on taking two or three bottles of water only to throw it up the next moment. Why, it's only just now that the priest has told me that the disease in my system is beginning to be washed out . . . which means I will have to take more and more of this water until I am cleaned. This priest! He had shown me some black matter, a small worm, and some larvae that came out of my bowels in proof of what the Abbo holy water is doing for me. But still, I can't go on taking bottles after bottles of water only to vomit it the next time and see some kind of proof. What is proof for me when I am disintegrating and losing the little energy I have left? Especially after what the *koso* water is doing to me. I've been taken twice now to that thorn-bush. And God knows what is coming out of my system – some pieces of my intestine, perhaps. And if it is not my intestine, I have no doubt it must be some parts of my heart or liver . . . and with nobody looking into it, not even Woynitu. And had it been because of its smell, this neglect! No, it smells no worse than that filthy air we had to breathe in that hut. But still, nobody cares. I should think that it is about time I tried to take care of myself. At my ripe age, I simply can't stand vomiting and excreting at the same time. No matter how much of my disease is coming out! I just can't. . . . Just look at him, that priest, with his incense-bearer swinging his copper vessel, still mumbling some prayer under his breath and making his mysterious passes over those bottles. I tell you I am not going to drink it even if refusing means my death. I hope to God that conjure-woman comes by and rescues me from that priest and those bottles. . . .

At least I know that by now she has got the white sheep ready for me. And I am expected to do nothing except allow them to anoint me with the blood or some other stuff. And as to the frequency and fluidity of my faeces, I hope she will have a way of stopping it. She will even look into it and tell me how much water, mucus, blood, and larvae I am secreting. Yes, I hope she will do just that – even if it be to brag about the efficacy of the roots she administered to me ... the white sheep – that I believe is my rescuer. I wish I had energy enough to kill it myself. . . . How many were they? Yes, five . . . with all the tarbush with a blue tassel at the end of a long string, the overcoat, blanket, cooking pots and canteen – those Italians. I was full of vigour and valour then. I wish I had now half the energy I had then . . . the fields dotted with the corpses of white men and mules, and locusts that were destroying nearly all the crops of the land . . . the bleak, cold, windswept and uninviting land of the North . . . I wish I had energy enough to kill that white sheep myself . . . and those robbers who encountered me on my retreat – just like these beggars and cursed devils, they think they can live on me. And all these priests seem to be one with them . . . have you fed me, clothed me, sheltered me and all that bit of nonsense. Ignorant as they are, they don't seem to know the promise that was given to Tekle Haymanot, 'Whoever is buried at your place will go directly to Heaven.' . . . and all that bit about sulphuric fire . . . it was meant to frighten me, I know – to make me squander my money on these good-for-nothings. . . . Certainly, this poverty is a punishment inflicted upon them by God for the sinful life they have lived working on saints' days and holidays. They should have been making fifty to one hundred genuflexions during their prayers for a whole year. And these others, the so-called townsmen and women, look at how they are eating their breakfast, displaying it like that as if they have got with them all the delicacies in the world – just look at him munching and nibbling from that bone – for all I know that mutton could have been knocking around on the market stalls for days in a row before it was bought – and he is trying to show it off to these poor beggars around him. I hope that conjure-woman comes along before that priest gets through his mumblings . . .

'Thou shalt live by the sweat of thy brow,' he said.

'I was governor of a district, but now I am a grain dealer,' I continued.

'The humbler the work the nearer to heaven we are,' he said.

'If grain was sold by the measure, I knocked at the sides of the *kunna* or *erbo* with my palm, and cleverly shifted the grain away from the edges,' I said.

'Blessed be He that gives us the power to be as gentle as the dove and as clever as the serpent,' he said.

'I made it stand up in a mound in the centre and slowly transferred it to my sack, helping the *kunna* by encircling it with my palm and fingers all around the edge,' I said.

'Blessed be He who forgives our shortcomings,' he said.

'If it was sold by the *sellecha*, I would pound it with a stick or my fist, in that way getting more than I paid for. . . .'

'Blessed be He that gives us insight into things,' he said.

'And if I were drawing up contracts, O, how clever I was, be it for the lease of my land or some other purpose, I always found a way to insert forfeit clauses, most of the time, taking advantage of my client's illiteracy. Some, of course, accused me of it, but it was of no help to them since they had to spend a lot of money on the officials only to lose the case at the end.'

'Blessed be He who gives us heart and mind to act in the way we do,' he said.

And so many other sins of mine I told him, to receive absolution. And what was the end of it all! That I should pay penance by contributing money for the repair work of a near-by church of St Mary's. Well, I was stunned and told him I would find another priest who would give me less penance. He was angry with me for a time and had even to leave me, only to return a little while later and start mumbling again over that basin and forcing bottles after bottles of blessed water down my throat. I am sure he will charge me ten to fifteen dollars for such a service too. What a penitence! Just look at him dipping his fingers in that basin and murmuring. Perhaps, he is going to be through with it in a moment. Oh, my God, at least there comes the peasant, and it must be that they have got the white sheep and are ready. . . .

Part Three

1 *Goytom*

Fitawrary lying here at the mercy of two men and a conjure-woman, and Woynitu standing beside him – I wish she weren't as beautiful as she looks now. And standing right over him, fanning him with a branch of *besanna* leaves. She looks like an angel. And the way she is looking at the kid – a bundle of rags – immovable and frightened. What is there interesting in him? Looks more dead to me than alive. Sitting immovable as he does, with his head drooping over his knees.

'Is he sleeping?' I whisper, meaning my father.

'No, he is fondling his pistol,' she says.

I wish I could fondle you the way he fondles his pistol. And the way she says 'fondling'. It sounds like you want to swallow it – sound and word and all – swallow it. She looks at the fireplace, her gold tooth shining. The fire reflecting on her face. You wouldn't think that she is sad and lonely, looking at her. She seems to smile in the fire light, and in daylight at that. Smiling at her troubles.

'You ought to rest your hand a little!' I say. Those little hands. It pains me to see them get tired. Fanning as she does. And Fitawrary breathing evenly when I know well enough that he is snoring. In his heart of hearts, I know he is snoring. And I know, he is doing his best to snore. I know that is the way of the men of title. And she tells me, he is not even asleep.

'He is asleep and he is snoring,' I whisper to Woynitu. Fitawrary clears his nose and his throat. I know he is snoring.

And then the sound of footsteps, and the peasant enters the hut. He doesn't look at the Fitawrary. And he doesn't look at me. But he looks at Woynitu. And with a smile too. Like the fire that smiles on her gold teeth. He smiles at her. And sitting by the fireside, he pinches at it with a stick. So hot as it is, the hut. He pinches at the fire – the peasant and the fire smiling at Woynitu. Fitawrary changes sides and sleeps with his face to the wall. He doesn't want the peasant and the fire to smile at him. And Woynitu smiling her disappointment away.

The wife goes out and comes in again. With cabbage leaves in her hand. Takes the circular *sefed* made of grass. Puts the cabbage on it and starts picking the leaves – now and again beating it on her left hand. To clean the dust and worms from each leaf. Beating it now and again. And putting the leaves in an earthen pot half full of water. And putting the pot on the three stones around the burning fire.

'These leaves are from my part of the garden,' says the peasant, 'they are for the market and you shouldn't have cut from those,' he says, taking one leaf and eating it raw. Then he looks around, and finding a gourd, dips it into the earthen jar of water and drinks. He takes some tobacco leaves from a knot tied at the edge of his home-spun cotton garment, mixes it with ashes from the fire and places it between the underlip and the lower front teeth.

'You shouldn't have cut those leaves,' he says, slowlike, and spitting air from his tobacco. 'And please add some pumpkin in the pot,' he continues. The wife doesn't even look at him. She takes a small stick and starts mixing the cabbage. Product of deep brown or black soil. Why? I ask. If this had been served in the wind-swept, uninviting part of Northern Shoa, I wouldn't have noticed it. But here, it is simply out of place. And this sudden spate of rain outside, from the heavy thunderstorm miles away in the interior. I think it's God's blessing. It sometimes washes down the bodies of cows, sheep and goats into the low countries. I wonder why it doesn't wash down all the crawling creatures from this mountain top. As when the flood comes at night and washes away the shep-herd or the travelling merchant who has encamped on a low level by the bed of a stream. I wonder why it doesn't? Or why the moun-tains do not shut all vestiges of breeze from these superfluous creatures of dogs and two-footed animals? Why doesn't the radiant heat that comes off the rocks burn them down? Or why doesn't the volcano erupt anew and flood the place north and south?

'You shouldn't have cut my cabbage,' says the peasant, spitting tiny drops of spittle into the air. And the sick woman sprawling in all directions. She thinks she has the hut all to herself. As if the Fitawrary is non-existent. As if Woynitu is not standing behind him protecting him from heat, flies, and the peasant. She is sprawling in every direction. And this peasant with his ugly mule tied outside! He thinks that he is also a Fitawrary. Just because he has a mule. Why should he want pumpkin added to his cabbage? Just because he owns a mule. And the way she is snorting. With all the sores on the withers, back, belly, and sides. I wish he had the ring-bit put in her mouth. And that wooden saddle at the corner. These two would have made her badly marked in the mouth and the back and she wouldn't have snorted as she is doing now. Trying to snore as if she is the Fitawrary . . .

I wonder what would have happened to this place if it had not been for the smell of the *Wanʒa* and *Koso* flowers. Everybody and everything would have smelt like a skunk. Except Woynitu, of course. She is a civet-cat. She has her musk to deliver her from the evil smell. I wish the rain would stop and I could run away from this place. I certainly am not going to kill the sheep at the sacrificial place. And I shouldn't be here when the Fitawrary awakes— But as it is, I can't go out. Sodden and watery as the landscape is now. I simply can't. Much as I would like to be under one of the golden mass of mimosa trees, on those wild flowers, I can't go out. I have to pass the time smelling like a skunk and feeling like a skunk. There it goes again, the thunder – reverberating from mountain to mountain. At least it has done some good. It has frightened Woynitu. And she is sitting now by her sick father. I wonder if she is thinking of our home in Addis. Stuffy as it is, this room. Our home with large beds and sheets and blankets. With cushions and covers of different coloured silk and the floor covered with Debre-berhan carpets. Silk curtains covering the doors and windows and the walls nicely plastered with all kinds of newspapers – *The New Era*, *The Voice* and *Today's Ethiopia*. I wonder if she is thinking of the comfort in our home.

'I'm hungry!' says the peasant.

'Put more tobacco under your tongue. It will drive off the hunger until the cabbage cools down,' answers the wife for the first time, with a quick decisiveness.

And my father starts to act like a trapped wild animal. He sits up for an instant and goes down on his back again, his eyes rolling in their sockets. He seems to writhe and twist in some kind of grip, his face gradually assuming blankness . . . oh, how I want to urinate, with the rain still pouring down and the mule snorting. It has even started to squeal, poor beast in the rain . . . but why should I care about the mule or the rain? Let it rain until it washes down everything. Let her squeal to her heart's content— I still want to go out and urinate in the rain – with the mule squealing and the rain pouring. It will be like being one with the sky. Urinating in the open. I wish Woynitu would feel that way too. I wish she would go out and be one with the sky. Feeling the way the sky feels. Feeling the way I feel. What does it matter if Fitawrary and the mule are snoring and snorting? What does it matter if the sick woman is sprawling in all directions? What does it mattter if the peasant and his woman are waiting for their cabbage to cool down? With us feeling one with the sky, everything will be all right!

2 The White Sheep

The sheep pulled with a silken cord tied around its neck, Fitawrary carried in a litter made of fresh boughs according to the instruction given by the conjure-woman, and shaded under an umbrella borrowed from St Mary's church, and the rest of the party – all set out towards the place of sacrifice.

'Baaa . . . baaa . . . baaa . . . ,' the sheep, and Fitawrary talking to the priest:

'If after all this, I die, I've arranged that everything be executed according to custom.'

'These days the will of the deceased is not very much respected.'

It is rumoured that the conjure-woman usually goes to this priest for advice in the curing of any ailment with which she is not familiar. That is why he has come with them after the blessing of the holy water for Fitawrary. As a matter of fact, the umbrella was his idea and he was even kind enough to hold it over Fitawrary.

'Not with me! Everything will be conducted according to my testament.'

'What I was actually implying was, people are not faithful to the memorials that used to be given in the olden days.'

'I've also dealt with them. As in the olden days, on the thirtieth day of my death, there will be a feast with abundance of provision, with one sheep exclusively for the priest, of course.'

'Oh...'

'On the fortieth day, two fat oxen, fifteen barrels of *tella*, five hundred pieces of *injera* . . . I've also allotted fifteen dollars for masses which will be held during the forty days. . . . On the eightieth day, two oxen, three sheep, twenty barrels of *tella*, one thousand pieces of *injera* will be prepared – and all for priests, scribes and some invited guests. The poor, of course, will have plenty to eat and drink. . . . And the big *teskar*, why! Six months later – I simply don't wish to talk about it now. You just wait and see . . .'

'May I ask where all this memorial feast is to take place?'

'At Debre-Libanos, of course, if everything is done according to my will.'

'And if not?'

'Why if not?! Of course I shall be buried at Debre-Libanos.'

'If it's not the will of God, I mean.'

'We have made provisions for that too . . . not only will the feast be conducted at the place where I will be buried, but also half of my wealth will go to it. And the rest to all the people who shall take part in the prayer for my salvation.'

'Does it mean any church other than Debre-Libanos?'

'Yes, any church.'

'Why then half of your wealth as well?'

'They may have to do a lot of praying to save my soul.'

'Have you heard that through the intercession of the blessed Virgin Mary, all can obtain salvation?'

'Yes, I have – why?'

'Well, as I told you, we have St Mary's church close by where I am head priest. You can have your salvation as easily here as at Debre-Libanos. If you want, I mean.'

'No, I still prefer Debre-Libanos. Thank you, however, for your suggestion.'

'May I ask what is weighing on your soul that much? I may be of help, you know.'

'Oh, a lot of things. . . . You know I was a district governor once. And it happened one year that I lost a very fat spayed sheep, like this one, in fact. Perhaps, that was bigger, I don't remember clearly. And so, I sent my servants throughout the district to search for him. But no sign of him was there. I was so infuriated. I didn't know what I was doing. You know, it wasn't the sheep that made me that angry. But the idea of it all – that a man, any man for that matter could have the arrogance to come to my place and steal my sheep. . . . Well, one day, it was fifteen days later, I remember, I was out to our market place for some other purpose. . . . And what do you think I came face to face with?'

'Your sheep, perhaps.'

'No, the skin of my sheep. . . . I came face to face with the skin of my sheep. . . . What came of it all is hard to tell. . . . Anyway, the culprit, a young lad of twenty was caught. We tried various means of punishment to extort the truth from him. And we succeeded, of course, at long last. . . . And as was the practice of the time, he was indicted, and I sentenced him to thirty lashes and a year's imprisonment. . . . Then, he was taken into the same market area for the punishment. Two men on either side of his hand held him by a long cord while another man brandishing his *jiraff* gave him the thirty lashes. I still hear his exclamations after every blow, *All ye who see me thus, profit by my example.* His skin got terribly scored by the *jiraff* . . . And after a month or thereabouts, he died in prison. . . .

'Well, I somehow can't get him out of my system.'

'But as you have said, he had admitted to his crime of theft.'

'I don't know, my friend, perhaps, there are some truths that you cannot extort by punishment.'

They reached the cross-roads where stood the naked tree whose crest had been blasted by lightning. They then brought down Fitawrary under some shady tree, stretched a white *shemma* to screen him from the group, and commenced to prepare the ground for the victim.

Goytom didn't show up; he had purposely avoided the occasion. The lot of killing the sheep, therefore, fell to the peasant.

The priest started to mumble some exorcism under his breath, made some passes over Fitawrary and the sheep, and the peasant, having sharpened his knife, dragged the sheep to the spot. Then, the preparation over, the sheep was killed and its blood was received in a basin to which were added all the contents of the entrails. Then all was thoroughly mixed up and the Fitawrary took off his clothes.

The idea of marking the Fitawrary's forehead with the blood of the victim had been abandoned for a better and more effective way of healing him – smearing and scrubbing him with the mixture to the accompaniment of a light beating with the tripe.

The conjure-woman and the priest started to administer the medicine.

The expression on Fitawrary's face was one of contortion and revulsion – he seemed to be repeating the one expression he couldn't get out of his system, *Oh ye, who see me thus.* . . .

3 *Woynitu*

His head is trembling. His hand is moving nervously over it. His face has gone ghastly dark. Only his eyes seem to be alive. Burning like red coals. When he breathes, the phlegm rattles in his chest. And from his throat comes a singing moan. Once in a while he sneezes violently and repeatedly. It takes him a long time to become himself again and to look around him. And I feel a great pity for him. It's very hard on me to look at him in that condition . . . a human marabou. An independent man who always makes his own decisions and goes his own way. It grieves me to see him being beaten with dirty tripe; the gold chain around his neck jumping on his chest and the gold cross on it – it grieves me. And the story of the young man who died in prison! Why is it that he feels it so painfully? As if it were he and not the young man who was lashed by the *jiraff*? As if it were his skin that got scored. As if it were he who actually died? My God, I don't understand these things. I don't understand them at all . . . I used to think of my mother as a living corpse. That her life isn't worth living at all. And yet my father is more dead than she . . . what is he trying to prove by being beaten with tripe? What is he trying to prove by bathing in blood and filth? And by smearing the gold cross on his chest? And what is the point of his living in this condition? Stripped of his belief, cleanliness, pride and everything else besides? And yet my mother also tries to live in that condition. She even tried to educate and clothe me in that condition . . . Why? Educate me to be what? To be like her or like my father or like both?

'You have at least your mother's face,' he tells me. But what if I have it, since the outcome of it all is to be employed in the service of the tavern. 'And you are like me in struggling to get what you want,' he says. But what is it that he wants that I want? And if he doesn't know what I want, how does he know I am like him in the struggle? Are my dreams, my wants, perhaps? Honestly I don't know what I want. If it is to live the way my mother lives or the way he lives – I'd rather die. Just look at that peasant! How he is looking at the dead sheep. Wide eyes gazing at it beneath his massive scowling forehead. And the priest and the conjure-woman arguing about the path they should take for the return trip.

'No, we can't go back the same way we came here,' says the conjure-woman.

'As long as we don't look back at the sacrificial sheep, it doesn't matter which way we take,' argues the priest.

There are so many goat-paths leading up to the top of the mountain – the longest and easiest one (for older people) goes round and round and round the mountain and comes up a little farther every time it makes a circle. Not much of a distance covered, though. (Eight times we had gone around the several hills yesterday when we came up to the top.) And then there are shorter and shorter ones, down to a distance of fifty to a hundred metres, for the adults, the youth, and the children – going steeper and steeper according to age and strength. And all of them going to the same place. And yet, in this blazing sun, they waste their time arguing about which path to take. Why they wouldn't take any one of the many paths is strange – I hope to God they wouldn't choose the longest or the steepest of the paths, though. I just don't think I can climb them today.

'Why don't we take that path?' suggests my father, pointing at it. He means the one for the children.

'No, that is too steep! Your servants will have a hard time climbing that,' answers the priest.

'When I was their age, I used to climb steeper hills with heavier loads on my shoulders,' he says.

59

Finally, the conjure-woman chooses the one for the adults, and we start moving upwards, carrying on our heads the burning furnace of the afternoon sun.

4 *The Prescription*

As they were returning from the sacrificial place, Fitawrary sounded as if he had awakened to reality for the first time during the pilgrimage.

'The climate, the soil, the water – everything here at the stretch of the hand. I don't really understand why everybody is poor and wretched around this place.' He was discussing things outside himself.

'People around here are lazy, that is why; they try to live on the bounties bestowed upon Abbo,' the priest answered him, when the conjure-woman intervened:

'Things are not what they look, sir. The people are poor because God has willed it that way.'

'Oh no, don't put the blame on God...,' the priest protested.

'Why shouldn't I? Isn't it He who brought on us all the calamities of the past months? Locusts destroyed our crops; then cattle disease broke out; and then to complete the misery, the summer and spring rains failed. . . . Surely, I'm not blaming Him for nothing.'

'And what has happened to the people who occupied the hamlets on the hillsides? Only very few people seem to be living in them. I don't even see smoke issuing from many of the huts. And many of them are in very bad condition – grass and weeds have grown everywhere; and the thorn and bushes that shut the enclosures are in bad repair. It seems there's something wrong with this whole area.'

'Many of them are uninhabited. Some of the farmers have gone to the near-by towns to work as porters, and some have taken to the highways trying to earn their living by levying blackmail on people.'

'And some have bought head-dresses and copper crosses and are posing as priests,' the priest added.

'And your animals are not good either for the farm or for the market.'

'They live only on what they pick, sir. When it is dry, they feed on dry grass. And when there is some rain, on the tender grass that springs shortly after it. Both ways, it's a problem to them. Especially the change from the dry food to wet and tender grass. It kills them in hundreds – bowel complaint and coughing.'

'You mean to tell me that they catch cold and die?'

'Yes, sir, when they are baked by the hot sun and then when immediately there is rain, they get drenched and catch cold.'

'And you do nothing to help them?'

'We try, sir. But the animals aren't brought to us on time.'

'The same thing happens to us people in the priesthood.'

'Don't tell me you are also drenched and baked.'

'Five or six times a year, we eat and drink to satiety. And the rest of the year we almost go hungry.'

'But you don't die because of it, do you?'

'Yes, many of us die. When a stomach that has known nothing but roasted peas and beans for months suddenly gets some juicy food, it cracks, and we die.'

'You should try first to get used to it by taking little by little.'

'But, you see, we eat when we get it or we may never get the like of it again.'

'But eat for the day not for the whole year at a time.'

'Yes, it's nobody but God to blame,' said the conjure-woman as if to herself.

'When giving alms and being charitable could have avoided the calamity, we simply sit back and blame it on God.'

'Abbo has led you to this place in time, sir,' she started again.

'Why do you say so?'

'Oh, haven't you seen those women on their way back from the water hole? They crossed us with their jars full of water.'

'Did they? No, I didn't see them.'

'That's a sign for your recovery.'

'It's the will of God, perhaps, that I live longer.'

Outside the conjure-woman's hut, a person with a broken leg

and a man with a sick mule were waiting for her return. Soon after the Fitawrary was taken into the hut and was made comfortable, she came out to attend to them.

The person with the broken leg was called first. The priest said some prayers over the leg, pronounced incantations, and the conjure-woman threw some sacred ash upon the wound. He was charged twenty-five cents for the service and left. Next came the mule. Some root was burnt and by holding it close to his nose, he was made to inhale the smoke; then, his feet were tied and he was thrown on the ground. And with a red-hot iron, three crosses were made on his skin – one on the back, another one on the ribs, and the third on the forehead. The animal, however, couldn't even rise from the ground at the end of it all.

The conjure-woman told the owner that he hadn't brought him soon enough.

Inside the hut the Fitawrary was irritated at finding some tobacco leaves by his *medeb* while he was trying to place his pistol, and was muttering to himself.

'Are you not comfortable on your *medeb*?'

'Why, a medicine woman, and you have tobacco leaves in your house? It's simply outrageous.'

'I sometimes use it for medicine. But it is mostly my husband who makes use of it.'

'Your husband?'

'Yes, he takes snuff.'

'Snuff?'

'He mixes the tobacco leaf with wood ash and . . . .'

'Eats it?!'

'No, he takes it into his mouth and places it between the underlip and lower front teeth.'

'What does he do that for?'

'It drives off hunger, prevents sickness and acts as a stimulant, sir.'

'For God's sake, take it away from my side.'

The deep rolling note of the ibis, which could almost be mistaken for the roaring of a lion, was heard near by.

'A good omen again,' commented the conjure-woman.

'You have good horns let into the walls. You could have used them for *wancha*.'

62

'Around here, we use gourds for drinking utensils.'

'I'll give your husband a gun – a good-looking breech-loader. . . . If I am well again, of course.'

'You will be well again. The ibis is always an undisputable sign of recovery.'

'How much do I have to pay in case I agree to your suggestion?'

'Which suggestion?'

'You said, if I wanted to, you would call the devils during the night and get from them. . . .'

'That costs you, of course. And as I have said, I can't do it all by myself. A lot of the work will be done by my friend here.'

'And the leather packets you have told me about?'

'They will contain wonder-working and mysterious ingredients and will be made according to the instructions we receive from the unnameables.'

'Well, I'll give it a thought.'

She called her son in to cut the throat of a red and white fowl and one of the servants was sent to throw it on a road that led in another direction – to misdirect the devils to another place, and prevent them from tracking down the sick.

5 *Woynitu*

I sit here on the floor beside my father's bed, my hands cupped beneath my chin and my body bent almost double and for no reason at all, I look up, and I see him motioning me towards him with his head. I stand up and go to him. He simply looks at me – stares at me – his eyes too small for his big face and the bald top of his head giving him a naked look, he looks at me without speaking. It is as though I am so empty that there isn't a feeling or thought in me . . . think he is struggling to find some way to begin, and then:

'I've got something for you,' he says, 'nothing much, but it will protect you against the evil eye,' and he fumbles with his shirt, and look away. Perhaps, it is the gold cross that he is looking for. He

63

must have seen me looking at it constantly at the sacrificial place. And then he takes it out from around his neck.

'I may not have long to live, and I hope . . .' and he finds it difficult to continue. I know he wants to live and I know he is afraid of death. And I don't feel sorry for him. 'Let me put it on your neck . . .' he starts again. I obediently bow to him and he puts it round my neck. And he kisses me on the forehead. He starts to speak again and swallows the words. I look at the cross, smeared as it is with the content of the sheep's stomach. I try to clean it with my finger-tips. The intricate pattern in the cross holds little particles of dust in its holes.

'I know it isn't much,' he starts again, 'and I know I haven't been much of a father, have I?' he says. With me trying to pick the dirt from the cross and he, speaking like this, it starts to give me a queer feeling.

'I have not been a responsible father,' he repeats himself. And being the man he is, I can't imagine any other way for him to be responsible. I start to pray that he live longer in order to be his other self. I start fondling the cross tenderly. Like the way he fondles his pistol. And I feel older all of a sudden. As though the pistol and the cross had something to do with it. The quietness grows longer and neither of us can say a word. And that is how I have sensed something about him. Not like learning a new fact. Something different. Something only the heart understands. Lonesome and old as he is. He can't have known any other way to breed children. And in his loneliness he must have chosen to be what he is. And now he feels like he is not much use to anybody.

Then he tells me about his money in the Addis Ababa Bank and about the houses he rents in the towns. And suddenly a bad cough seizes him and he struggles to overcome it. And when he does, his face stiffens and takes on a darkish pallor. His eyes become fixed and rigid again – the skin of his forehead gathering into wrinkles and folds. Some time passes. And then, as if from a reservoir of his energy, heavy words start pouring forth one after another. Words throbbing with yearning and wrath. And he stops just as suddenly.

It seems he must have been trying to tell me about how things would have been if only he had lived some more years ... He is feeling sleepy now and I think I had better go out of this stuffy place into the bush and into the fresh air.

6 The Peasant

Well, I couldn't help it. I had to return here by another road. Oh, sure, I'm a working man. I can't see all this good meat go to the devils. Yes, I'm a working man. ...

I make the circular plough from the tough wood of the mimosa tree, and bore a hole at the centre of its curve. I make the two flat supports of tough wood, which will be placed on either side of the hole. I buy the iron plough-share that I place between the supports, and with the raw hide which I again buy, I bind all the parts together to the shaft. Then, I make the yoke from lighter wood, not from tough wood, no – tough wood would be an extra load for the oxen to carry – but from lighter wood. I make it round, smooth, and comfortable too, so that it doesn't chafe the shoulders of my oxen. Then, I bore four holes, two on each side of it. I make four round sticks which are put through the holes to attach the animals to the yoke. I make also the handle of the whip from tough wood – smooth and good looking. And I buy the leather.

Oh, me, don't I know my business? I make also the iron hoes. And how have I come to know all these skills? I learnt them all by myself. But my woman! She knows only what is given her of God. If God had given the gift to me, I would have been as good and respected a conjure-woman as she is. But now as it stands, He hasn't given it to me. She is the conjure-woman. And I am not. And perhaps, I don't want to be one, because I know what I am doing and she doesn't. Let her be all the conjure-woman she likes all her life, I don't care. I am also a conjure-ploughman. Yes, I am.

Oh, no one will get me. I know. Not even the Fitawrary – determined as he is to take my conjure-woman to Addis. ... I doubt if she would ever come back. A rich Fitawrary and a man of blood, a gentleman who knows how to talk with his big men. Well, I don't blame him. Something in him must have told him that she is a real conjure-woman. And real ones are harder and harder to come by these days. But she has told me herself that she gets her conjuring ability from Abbo and that she might lose it if she goes from Abbo's neighbourhood. Well, I don't blame her or him. . . .

The way he was looking at her as though he loved her. Why, I love her as well because she is a conjure-woman. And I think, she loves me because I am a good conjure-ploughman.

Ayeeeeeeeye! this sheep I am skinning now, how fat and delicious it is. A bite of it will fill your mouth with fatty juice. But my woman, she never allows me to take it to our hut. It's for the devils, she says. The devils in eating the fatty meat will forget to torture the Fitawrary, she says. But being what I am, I don't have the heart to see good, tasty meat go to the devils alone -- let alone such juicy meat as a spayed sheep's. Oh, perhaps, one wonders if I am not eating the meat in order to kill the Fitawrary. No, I have no intention of doing that. I need him alive. I want him to come as often as he pleases to my conjure-woman. Oh me! I love juicy meat. I hope to God that Fitawrary is cured. Then, true as this meat, he will tell the people in Addis about the wonder of my woman's healing powers. And more and more people will come. And more and more meat I will get. And my conjure-woman, of course, will have more and more grain. . . .

Speaking of grain, ha! ha! I do everything by myself. I do the farming, the sowing and the hoeing by myself. I keep the ditches clear so that the water during heavy rains shall run away to the streams as quickly as possible. I won't let it swamp my farms, no – by no means. I spend long hours of my days removing weeds from the growing grain with my hands. I cut, cock, and stack my crops with my own hands. I make my own *wudemma* by making a large circle. I pile neat little bundles of dry grass at intervals of about ten hands around the threshing floor. I burn the bundles down to ashes. I place the leaves of *besanna* on the ashes and a stone on each of them. Sometimes, I do such things even on the foot paths leading to the floor. This way, safe against interference from the demons, I'll be sure of a good harvest and I arrange the crop on it. And with the help of my ox and my donkey, I start to tread out the grain. Then, I do the winnowing by throwing the grain in the air in small quantities so that the husks can be blown away by the wind. And what does she do in return for all this? She does only what is given her of God. And she doesn't even allow me to take this good meat to my own house. One can't imagine such a thing to happen to me, can one? With all the energy I put in everything!

I am even the one who builds the wicker granaries. I build them and plaster them with clay with my own two hands – to prevent the rats and mice from eating the grain. I build also the underground pits for our millet and corn. I cement their insides with mud made of the mounds of white ants. I dry them thoroughly. And I put in the grains myself. Ow! other men force their women to do all these things with them. But me – no! I let her do only her conjure-work. And in return, she doesn't even allow me to take this good meat into my own house.

She even refuses sometimes to grind the flour, to brew the *tella*, to pick raw cotton from the seeds and spin them into threads, to go to the weekly market with farm produce, even to cook my food, collect sticks for the fire, and to come down to this stream to fetch water. She says carrying the heavy water-pots on the back spoils her ability of conjuring. And at such times . . . who can believe this? I'm forced to do them for her. And to what end? She won't even allow me to take this good fat meat into my own house. And I eat it raw most of the time.

That meat is for the devil, she says. And I say, so be it, if he comes I will let him have his share. And I wait and wait for him, but he doesn't come. And so I take it all for myself. Perhaps it is too small for him, most of the time – a bullock may be is his idea of a feast. I don't know. But me – no! I get such a chance only two or three times a year. On such occasions like these or when an animal falls over a cliff and dies. Fat, good meat of a spayed sheep doesn't often come my way. And so, I don't let such a chance slip by.

Oh, yes, sometimes she calls me a lout – just because I love to eat raw meat. 'Some day you might even eat me raw,' she says – if there is famine or something like that, she means. I don't know. I might. As if I didn't want to carry away that beautiful woman of the Fitawrary's! She is so beautiful, you feel like swallowing her whole. Wow! I might. I mean, when I see beautiful things I get the appetite. I feel a gnawing something in my stomach. I feel like eating them up . . . swallowing them whole, or something like that. Well, I might, I say. And she smiles and comes nearer to me and embraces me. Like saying, 'Oh – no, please don't do it. Let me be only your conjure-woman.' And conjurer as she is, she has a way of saying it, like the way she wants me to make it hot for her. Well, what could I do? I simply let her be. But for all that, she wouldn't even allow me to take this good meat into my own house. And that makes me want to eat her up all the more. . . .

Chechechecha! How I love to hang the meat over my *medeb* and enjoy looking at it, and sometimes, when I feel like eating it simply grab a piece. But – no! She doesn't understand. She simply is mixing up everything.

Fitawrary thinks the devil will soon be wolfing his sheep and that he will be cured in due time; my woman thinks the devil is eating it with me; and I think I am eating it all alone. Alone by this clear stream. Perhaps some think that it is hell to eat a thing like that alone. Not even sharing it with one's own son and woman. And don't I have the problem of eating it all soon! And besides, I'll have to go up to Abbo to pray – to tell him about my little sins, my plans, and the difficulty that preacher of his is causing me.

I hope Abbo will tell me something in my dream before his anniversary tomorrow.

And my landlady, asking me to help her to build that *das* – I don't think I can make it for her before noon. . . .

Well, I hope I'll eat half of this meat before lunch. I hope I will finish it in two meals and be at home by the evening – before the evening service at the church, perhaps. To be frank, I can finish it in one meal if I really try to. But I am planning to eat it slow – to enjoy it, to really enjoy it. And besides, I always enjoy the thrill in the woods. Even if it means passing the night here, I mean. You have always got company, and no ordinary company at that – the jackals, the hyenas – they all keep you company, hoping that you would throw them a bone or two. And what a noise they make. Sort of frightening. The jackals with their weird cry and the hyenas calling to each other until the dogs of the area assemble and drive them off with their yelping. A real thrill. . . .

And everybody about this place trying to feel grown-up – with guns and things. And poor me, what do I have? I don't have anything. The good thing is that the poor beasts don't happen to know it. They are afraid of me. But if they did know that I don't have even two oxen of my own, they would have got me on one of my outings. And all because my conjure-woman is always up to feeding devils and not feeding me. She doesn't charge enough money for her conjuring. She doesn't. . . .

Oh, what delicious meat this is! And how things change . . . this tongue which I'm now eating, for example, used to go to the master of the house . . . how tasty it is! I never had a chance to have a mouthful of it then. Oh, how delicious . . . this rump – it was also the master's . . . and this fatty strip of backbone – also the master's . . . and these thick ribs. How tasty they would be if they were broiled on the embers of a wood-fire. How much I would have liked to make a fire! But then, it would attract strangers and that would be bad for my woman . . . and this meat near the belly, again for the master. How many times I used to swallow my saliva when it used to be my turn to put this meat on the embers of a wood-fire for him. And he never seemed to have eyes for my languishing appetite . . . and this chest, my favourite part of all – I wish all meat had a delicate strip like this – again for the master. How tasty it looked when he ate it boiled . . . and this gristle from the chest, again my favourite, it used to go to that entertainer . . . and this meat down the hip-bone, again to the master, not even a mouthful of it to us, the servants . . . and the delicate inside part of the thighs, again to the master . . . and this beautiful *cheguarra* – what a delicacy is tripe and liver cut into pieces and mixed with the contents of gall-bladder squeezed over it – and how the master loved it for his first serving . . . it is a bit spoiled though now – crazy people, beating the Fitawrary with it – a bit spoiled . . . and poor creatures as we were, left only with the remains – these two *mahlagedas*, for example, went to the washer and the shield bearer – real good arms with lots of meat . . . this neck, paunch, and this bit of liver, to the grass cutter . . . and this *shim-fella* – it should have been good, being near the tripe, but as it is, not good at all – to the cooks . . . and this fat membrane of the belly, and this bone, with a little bit of meat from here – what delicious shoulders this sheep has got – ayeee! You don't have to chew it more han twice to swallow – it simply melts – yes, this used to be mine the porter. . . .

t But now, well, everything is mine. I'm master and servant. I'm not full master yet – my woman doesn't allow me to take such mouth-filling meat to my own house. And yet, master as far as the meat is concerned. Of course, I can take it in by force, if I want to. Yes, I can. But that's not wise. She might tell the Fitawrary about it in her fury. And on top of that, if he died, I might be held responsible for his death. And so, what could I do? I have to make the best of it. And I hope I'll be able to finish eating the whole lot by tomorrow morning. And by then, who knows? Fitawrary may need another sheep – black one or red one, as the case may be. Who knows!

He collected all the meat on the sheep skin and carefully and delicately carried it closer to the stream.

The flies buzzed around his bundle and settled on his face in swarms. He tried to kill some of them, but it was an unequal combat. He seemed to have decided on something – stood up, cut a branch of *besanna* with a few leaves, sat down again. He put the branch on his lap, took his knife, cut a good lump of meat, filled his mouth to the lips, and started munching blissfully. . . .

Languidly picking up the branch once in a while and waving it backwards and forwards, backwards . . .

Part Four

1 The Landlady

The landlady had arrived late in the morning and with her little lady friend and retainers was already busy arranging for the memorial feast.

In the yard of one of her more prosperous peasants near the church, a big *das* with a framework of stakes was erected. Uprights were driven into the ground and horizontals fastened to them by ligaments of bark and supple shoots of trees. Green branches, sheep and other animal skins were thrown over it to protect the interior from the sun. At its centre, a strong post of timber was planted, with many stakes jutting out at right angles, on which was hung the meat of a cow covered with red cloth. The inside was lined with bamboo tables. At one corner were other lines of earthen jars of *tella* and at another piles of *injera* and some pots of *wot*. And its floor was carpeted with fresh grass and leaves. At the gate, a man armed with a long stick was standing – to show people their places, to make way for newcomers by dismissing old ones in time, and to keep order by guarding the entrance against the mob of beggars outside.

At the side of the *das* stood the peasant's hovel; and in front of it a small open space, strewn about with heaps of dung and rubbish, half overgrown with weeds. And greyish, blackish, ragged beings, their drivelling, crouching forms scarcely distinguishable from their surroundings, were waiting and yawning with their sheep-skin bags held up, for some remains of food. At their feet dirty water gurgled between the lumps of frozen manure.

Cocks and hens which were roosting in the hovel were moved to uneasy fluttering and clawing. Some sheep darted away in terror from the hullabaloo, their hoofs pattering over the frozen dung, and a dog whined loudly, then growled in angry alarm, and finally barked ferociously at the intruders. It seemed it was no torment to them to live where nothing changed year after year. The longer they lived the more compatible had the immobility of the environment become.

Outside the yard, on the mounds of manure on which light green grass sprouted, some better-looking peasants were sitting. They sat there as if held up from behind, a bunch of leathern-mannikins, outstretched arms and forward-hanging heads. Some of them looked totally crushed, uprooted from their barren and exhausted lands of the North. Glancing about them with dull, despondent eyes, they looked like the homeless dogs of the neighbourhood collected outside the yard. They all looked alike, and like the human beings around them, without hustling or growling, awaited the hour when a maid would throw them the refuse of the meal.

In the sky, the hawks were manœuvring. They didn't flutter about and squeak. They simply waited.

At the foot of a near-by tree, a bearded blind old man played the *masinqo*. A speechless grief quivered in his eyes and on his lips, which were convulsively pressed together, tensed against the gentle thrumming of the instrument. A bird sitting in the tree fluttered twice from branch to branch with a whistle, then jerking its tail flew up towards the church.

The landlady came out with some food carried by a maiden, with a man following her. A commotion broke out immediately. Everyone shouted at the top of his voice, gabbling two words to the other's one, the lady complained at a beggar smoking a cigarette. He was a miserable-looking fellow, wearing a woman's overcoat, which had patches all over the place – in front, down the back, and round the sides – was shorn of hooks, and torn into strips round the edges. He threw down the butt and stamped it out, afraid of losing his share of the feast.

Two lepers quarrelled over a place at the gate their blows smacking, smashing, regularly on one another. One of them fell flat on his face, struggling, kicking and puffing up the dust. He managed to pull himself up, and again they came to grips, squeezing one another with all their strength, till their ribs cracked. Each encountered the other's elbow, a head, or just empty air; one skipped round the other, caught him suddenly by the neck or leg in a grip like a vice; and the crowd round about laughed, whistled, neighed, applauded one or the other. One of the men was especially skilful in evading every attempt to be caught, dodging with incredible agility. They both fought heroically.

The food, however, was not for them but for those outside the yard.

2 Goytom

Kicking my heels about in the forecourt of the church, I waited for my group to return from the sacrificial place. I thought about how life here was moving in its own way; the pledges of sheep and goats to Abbo tethered in a corner of the yard were bleating incessantly; horses standing by the gate were flicking away the troublesome flies with their tails; the owners sitting near the fence were leisurely prodding the dirt from their feet with their whips; the preacher was praying fervently, then he began purposefully to splash the holy water from a bucket on a sick man; a man at a secluded spot was roasting some ears of corn on the embers of a wood fire, and catching my eyes with his (he must have taken me for an evil eye), came immediately towards me and lowering his *shemma* so as to leave the shoulders bare, a sign of respect and humility, offered me to eat to the accompaniment of, 'I have seen more than one great fortune slip by into chinks and clefts . . .' I knew that if I allowed him to talk he would go on for ever. So I pretended to be engrossed in my own problems and politely refused his offer. . . . 'I'm going to reap a good harvest though this year . . . ,' he was still saying. He seemed to realize at long last that I was not in the mood and hesitatingly returned to his fire and corn. And my eyes flitted from him to the fence – masses of nettles had squeezed their way under it; docks had thrust up their heads through its torn parts to catch, it seemed, at the legs or the skirts of the passers-by; and under the canopy of the inside part of the gate,was faded writing on a long stretch of *abujedid*, 'Welcome, Your Imperial Majesty.'

Yes, you have helped me to see the light, I was thinking –
    'How come I have such a weakling for a son after all I have done for you . . . ?'
    'You brought me up that way,' I say.
    'Haven't I educated you?' he asks.
    'Yes, you have,' I answer.
    'Haven't I insisted on your continuing your education?'
    'Yes, you have.'

'And when you quit school, didn't I find you a good job?'

'I didn't consider it so.'

'Why not?!'

'Well, I didn't want a job that I got through your friends.'

'Why didn't you get one for yourself then?'

'I couldn't, the way things were.'

'Oh, you couldn't! You know why?'

'Yes, I do.'

'It's because you know nothing.'

'I know nothing?!'

'Yes, nothing.'

'Your idea of work is perhaps sitting in an office and copying letters, drinking cups after cups of coffee and gossiping.'

'Whatever pays is work as far as I am concerned.'

'As far as you are concerned!'

'Perhaps your idea of work is feeding on me like a vulture.'

'You forget that I am my mother's sole inheritor.'

'Oh no! You are not. It's first mine as long as I live.'

'I hope to God you live as long as you abhor living.'

'You leave that worry to me, and besides that's none of your business.'

And, of course, I left that worry to him – only to end up here.

What a man he is! What he is made of is indeed stern stuff. The way he went on vomiting and excreting at the same time! And still his old unchanging self. How he hated to be treated like a sick man, let alone like an old man. I hope I live as long as he has lived, only to know what a disgusting jelly I would change to. I'm sure I won't even lead a decent vegetative life by then. I may disintegrate. I hope I will still have guts enough to kill myself . . . Oh, no – not him. He would rather vegetate and disintegrate. He would rather go on talking about things dead and buried:

'When I was your age I used to walk ninety kilometres a day . . . when I was your age, I used to kill a sheep by myself, with every part of the meat cut from its proper place. . . . I used to saddle a horse, load a donkey, eat like a man, drink like a man, fight like a man, love like a man . . . and look at you,' he says.

Perhaps he is right. I don't know how to do all those things in his style. I don't like raw meat, for instance, nor do I need to know how to saddle a horse or load a donkey. And yet he doesn't seem to understand when I am up to something I need and to something I like doing. He goes on lecturing me on things I haven't got the slightest interest in. 'At the battles of Maichew, and Korem, when we ran short of rations we were forced to eat raw horse meat and drink the urine of our animals, and man, if I were the choosy type you are, I wouldn't have come out of those places alive. . . .'

Well, what was the point of arguing with him. For him survival is what matters – even if it means doing things that he under normal circumstances couldn't have done. But not to me! I'd rather die. And I hope to God he gives me the guts to act at such a time.

And haven't I seen that picture of a battle scene he hangs on the wall above his bed. All that rubbish in one picture: cavalry charge, mounted infantry and phalanx, all in action – shooting, spearing, shielding, hand-to-hand fighting – and hundreds of the white men dead and not even one Ethiopian. What an outrageous lie and how ridiculous! And he tells me that he has this and that medallion, as if I care a dot about it. Medallions given to people for telling the greatest of lies or for being the greatest of cowards. He expects me to take him as a hero! Why should I tell him that heroes are dead and buried? Why should I tell him that bravado is his wrong word for fear? And that he sometimes succeeded by sheer accident. Why should I tell him that medallions most of the time disguise a cowardly heart? No, let him wallow in the memory of his cowardice and hypocrisy. Let him go on blaming the young generation:

'Some of your lot, the so-called intelligentsia, know nothing but how to kill themselves. Food is no good, they go out and kill themselves . . . no work to do, they go out and kill themselves . . . no beautiful girl, no automobile, no villa, they go out and kill themselves. You and your kind are good-for-nothing, I tell you. Nobody of my generation would have done such silly things. Even if it was necessary, they killed themselves only after having killed their enemies. But just look at you! I don't think you are even capable of that. I don't think you can kill yourself like your fellow educated men. . . .'

Well, what could I have said to all that? Prove to him by killing myself, perhaps? Oh, no! I am not that crazy yet. I love life just as much as he does, perhaps in a different and better way. I love life only as long as I have all my senses intact. As long as I can contribute to the accomplishments of my fellow men. As long as I can love, hate, get angry, become merciful – as long as I feel the fire of life in me.

To imagine that he has lived at all! A man who has never loved for love's sake, who hasn't worked for work's sake, a man who hasn't fought for humanity, who hasn't stood for some universal truth in life, except – land, wealth, title, patriotism and that sort of rubbish. He tells me he has lived. And I tell him he hasn't. . . . And what is the end of it all? He believes the *ferenj* have bewitched me. He thinks that I am berserk or something. And he expects me to go to these priests for some charm or a little holy water to cure this Fitawrary-made complaint. And I say to hell with everything– the Fitawrary, the complaint, and the cure.

' . . . You have a rich land and much of every sort of natural produce,' this preacher was shouting as if he did not know that I don't own even a square yard of barren earth. And the idea that I can be rich by simply scratching the generous soil – why? Scratching has only led to poverty, more scratching to utter poverty. He need only go down from his pedestal of a church and enter one of those hovels. He will be welcomed by a high carnival of rats racing, playing, and squeaking and running over him the whole day and night. . . .

I hope to God the white sheep does him some good and that he lives long enough to hate his life of waiting for death.

3 The Peasant

And here now I meet this preacher splashing Abbo's water on the sick man and making money out of it. It's good he hasn't heard about the spayed sheep. He would have snatched it from me in no time. . . . But now, I tell him that I'm no ordinary ploughman – half of the sheep bulging in my stomach and the other half safely put away by your gate at my disposal. Well, as you see, I'm not trying to hide anything from you, Abbo – even those ears of corn I hacked from the preacher's farm. And I think I have come to you in time for you to think it over before your anniversary tomorrow.

Yes I have . . . and my landlady – she thought I wanted some of her meat in the *das*. 'You come here to fill your stomach,' she says; 'you didn't come to help us to erect the *das*,' she says; 'you sit out there with the rest of the peasants,' she says. And I simply come straight to you. Who wants her cow meat, anyway? A dead cow or something, she has for meat. As if I'm not known to eat spayed sheep. As if I care for her meat. And like an ordinary peasant, she wants me to sit outside. Who does she think she is? A Fitawrary or something? As if I'd care even if she were. . . .

'No, you are not allowed to come into the hut,' she says – my woman. Even without the meat of the spayed sheep. 'You will become a shadow to the sick man,' she says. A shadow! As if I am not all meat and blood. 'You throw your shadow on Fitawrary, and there is no chance of his recovery,' she says. And I tell her that I have heard a crow cawing – a sure sign that someone would soon die and be buried. And she tells me it cawed for the sick woman in our house. And I ask her if she is dead. And she tells me her relatives have taken her to her home. They take her to her home instead of burying her.

Fools! as if I didn't hear the crow cawing.

I have come to you in time, anyway. To tell you of my problems. For as you can see, my woman makes me angry most of the time. And I hope you will understand that I hacked off those ears of corn in my attempt to feed my child. She would not even allow him into the hut, telling him he would become a shadow too. Just because he is my son and I let him have some mouthfuls of meat. . . . Of course, I have left this preacher at least one ear of corn on each stem. I haven't hacked them all off.

And I feel that I am not altogether bad. . . .

And for those I left uncut at least, I hope you will turn your face towards me. And for the future, I have my plans which I hope you will like. . . I shall widen my fence and let pilgrims pass their nights in my yard. But not as I am now, of course. You know very well that I am too cramped, my hedge is too small and I don't have my own land to widen it . . . but I have the plan. And the plan will make me manage somehow . . . I hope you will not be angry with me, if I plant the landmark at my fence a little farther – that way, I will give the beggars a chance. I will let them pass the night in my fence . . . Oh, Abbo, just make a gesture with your hand, that way, sending lightning on that tree which has become a hindrance to my removing the landmark. Or, perhaps, make me dream tonight, teach me something that will help me destroy that tree. . . . If you but tell me in my dream tonight, I will know that you are with me and that you have forgiven me for those ears of corn. Or, perhaps, if you tell my neighbour to be kinder to me. . . . And here as he is splashing that water and making more and more money, I am sure he would not mind doing a small favour to you, I mean to me – with all those things that you are doing for him. Just tell him through the sick man he is trying to heal, he will understand that it is you speaking. . . . And with the way things are, always sending his cows into my *tef* and I, always chasing them out. . . .

And when in turn, my cow or sheep strays into his farm or if my calf breaks into his meadow, how he accuses me and makes me pay fines. . . . And that disciple-attendant of his, trying to be a preacher like him, he would turn the flock out into my *tef*, and the mule would somehow get into my corn at night – again and again - you know, and what did I do? I drove them out and overlooked the matter. . . . Oh, what a crook he is. I can't stand him any more. And a monk on top of it all. He shouldn't care for earthly things, no – he shouldn't. . . . Only recently, I lost my temper, I couldn't help it. And I laid a complaint before the district court – and what a sheepskin bag of *tef* I took to the judge. . . .

Yes, now, he is afraid of me. He wants to be friendly with me. . . . Oh, God, remember me in Your Holy Country, for as You know, it's my own land that I sow, my own hay that I reap, my own cabbage that I cut, my own firewood that I gather, and my own cattle that I graze. . . .

A woman, wizened as a chip of wood, whose head and swollen cheek were wrapped in an *angetlebse*, came along and began praying – mumbling various supplications under her breath, seeking all kinds of privileges and graces . . .

'I have come on foot all the way from Nazareth . . .' She was trying to enter into conversation with the peasant, 'If you are a native of this place, I would like very much to rent a lodging from you for a night. . . .'

'Abbo's anniversary is tomorrow, you shouldn't have come today.' Not at all pleased with her intrusion, he tried to wave her away from his side. But the woman wasn't ready to be brushed away like that and added . . .

'If you are willing, I'll pay you for the lodging.'

'I believe you have something with you for Abbo.'

'Yes, I have – fifteen dollars' worth of an umbrella.'

'Incense, wicks and candles as well?'

'Yes, I have some of each.'

'Then, perhaps, I'll consider having you for the night.'

'Thank you, man of God, thank you.'

'Well, what can one do? It doesn't seem to be Abbo's will. You see, I was out of my house to get some pat of butter for my blistering head. And here you come straight to me to give you a shelter. What can I do but return?'

'Oh, no, I don't want you to go to all that trouble. I will wait for you here until you come back.'

'What about the umbrella and things, with beggars and thieves all over the place, you might want to keep them in safe hands.'

'I have done that already.'

'The umbrellas and things? You have kept them with somebody?'

'Yes, I have.'

'May I ask with whom?'

'Who else, with Abbo, of course. I have already handed them over to that holy man.'

'The preacher, you mean?'

'The one pouring the water on the sick man.'

'You should then have asked him for a lodging, my dear woman. A man of his type must always have a place for people like you. And good-day to you. . . .'

'I don't understand you.'

'Oh, I know you don't. Only Abbo understands me.'

Suddenly, there started a commotion. A man was heard calling another man a thief; then, a struggle and exchange of blows followed. One of the men, a weak and weary looking beggar, couldn't maintain his balance; he fell full length, let out a shriek of horror, and like one demented, with his eyes closed, went down the steps on all fours backwards, sliding rather than running. He had been found stealing a hunk of bread wrapped in a cloth, stuck in the girth of one of the horses.

They caught up with him and the beggar started swearing, trying hopelessly to avoid the beating: 'May I fall through the ground here, if I have tried to steal anything. . . .' He was trying at the same time to wipe off a red smudge that disfigured his nose just under his eye.

'God, at least, give these men heart enough to help their fellow man. And help me, oh God, to collect twenty cents to clear off a little debt I owe for the stitching of my coat,' another beggar was saying, not disturbed at all by the hullabaloo and busily scratching at his badly chafed and bruised feet.

'You don't know, man, you don't know what to beg for – beg of God to strengthen in you the feelings of revenge, the feelings of hatred and disdain for these men. Pray to God to give you the courage to snatch . . . these are what count as long as you live. . . .' said the peasant lifting his bundle of meat on to his head, 'Yes, pray that God give you strength to avenge on your enemies – to wipe out the insult heaped upon you with your blood. . . .'

The owner of the hunk of bread struggled with the thief, trying to extort the truth by putting little sticks between his fingers, winding a strap round their ends and drawing them very tight. And when that didn't work, he gave the beggar's arm a good twist behind his back. The beggar, however, wouldn't budge, and the group agreed finally to deliver him over to Abbo to do as he saw fit.

The beggar seemed to have lost his wits after the beating he had received, and started shouting anew as soon as he was released: 'Don't kill me, brothers! Have mercy upon me, for Christ's sake. I haven't done anything . . . he can go and check his saddle now, if he wants! Only let me go away, and expiate my sinful wish and save my soul through prayer. I'll go on a pilgrimage from church to church, if you want me, or I'll remain hidden in some forest my life long. . . .'

The preacher left his task of splashing water on the sick man, and came to the group to settle the dispute. Many of them doffed their hats to him and kissed the silver cross he was holding. He then eyed the people right and left, assumed a studied air of decorum, screwed up his face like someone whose *tef* had been trodden on, and gave the alleged thief a good drubbing with words. Staring at him, his eyes nearly popping out of his head, and comfortably placing himself in the middle of the group, he began to preach in the name of Christianity:

'Yes, what he was saying was in a way right. In fear for their souls, there are many who have left the life of the world and have gone to hide in the forest and caves. There are many who abandoned their world for the wild things of nature. . . .'

The peasant meanwhile was telling one of the men in the group that the preacher had always eight ricks of cereals standing before his cottage.

' . . . Don't covet your neighbours' goods – don't try to take what is not rightly yours, for if you do, woe is all you will gain in the end . . . On that dread day of judgement the devils will make it hot for you with their iron pitchforks, yes, they will make it hot for you. . . .'

4 The Memorial Feast

The priests preferred to be by themselves and had long ago been shown to the hovel and were making merry. You could see them swollen with affected melancholy and swaying their head-dresses, and hear them smattering their snatched *Zeez* sayings in their Amharic conversation. Drinking and eating to excess, they seemed as if they were hoping to make themselves numb, to get rid at last of whatever was torturing them. It was a long while later that the other guests – the deacons, the scribes, the more prosperous-looking peasants of the village and some merchants and government clerks from the town – were shown to the *das*. And even then, they had to wait, squatting uncomfortably on both sides of the bamboo tables, for one of the priests to come along and say his blessing over the food and *tella* pots and give the people permission to eat and drink.

Once the blessing was done, however, the servants began immediately passing back and forth, carrying jars after jars of *tella*, pots of *wot* and great joints of raw meat. Great quantities of each were consumed in no time.

Then, before vacating the place for the next group, some of the elderly men stood up, and, gesticulating with their arms and putting on facial expressions of tragedy and loss, spoke a great deal on the valour of the deceased, and left, thanking and blessing the lady for having prepared such a grand feast in memory of her late husband.

The group comprising the poor people of the area came in next; and after them, the servants and farm-hands. In the meantime, the *agafari* at the door was lashing the beggars with his whip and dragging them out when they attempted to sneak into the *das*. It looked as if the beggars must have been waiting for this chance, for as soon as they saw their companions being beaten, they raised such a hullabaloo of vituperation against the lady and the deceased, it was as if pandemonium had got loose.

Inside the hovel, there was another kind of commotion. Some of the priests were growing more and more befuddled, their eyes staring unwinkingly at the opposite wall, with its lower part brown with cow-dung and its upper part plastered over with patches of dirt and mould. Some of them were clamouring and shouting without knowing either what they said themselves or what their companions were saying . . . shouting amidst that stagnation, the walls reeking with manure, the earthen floor with damp, and the *medebs* with sweat and rags and sheep- and goatskins. And yet none of them noticing it, none of them feeling it – completely befuddled. Even the flies seemed to understand the condition of the priests. Swarming in the sticky puddles on the wicker table or landing over the men's beards and faces and flexing their legs, they were having a good time. They were disturbed only when one of the priests gesticulated or sneezed or clapped his hands for more drinks, when they would rise in clouds of fury. Otherwise they seemed contented with what fate had ordained them to have.

Some of the beggars, realizing what was taking place inside the hovel, started elbowing each other, glueing their faces to the crevices in the wall. A priest who happened to see the intrusion got angry, and, trying to chase them away, walked through the heap of cow-dung and fell on his side, his threatening speech giving way to a string of curses and maledictions.

Late in the afternoon, a great pile of left-overs was collected in big baskets, and taken out for the beggars. At one corner, a beggar who found it troublesome to eat from this muddle of food on account of the bones in it, declared to a near-by friend that he wasn't hungry after all. His friend, however, had swallowed a juicy lump of meat in too great a hurry, got it stuck in his throat, and was turned deathly pale, twisting around in the dust in a fruitless attempt to get rid of the obstacle. The first man, when he saw the affliction, hit him on the nape of the neck, and the meat shot out of his throat right into the mouth of a near-by dog. 'A lucky dog!' murmured the beggar.

'I'll pull the skin over your ears for taking my share!' The two lepers were still picking quarrels.

Most of the beggars, however, had already gone up to the church and there were only four or five around: one of them was gathering the crumbs of *injera* and bread from his cloth to his palm; another was rummaging and picking lice out of the folds of his shirt and trousers; and another one seemed to have difficulty standing up. He fell, rose heavily from the dirt, and left the place swaying weirdly and jerking his feet. The rest waited for additional left-overs.

A basket of gnawed bones was then thrown to the dogs, whose whimpers and bawls echoed all over the place. Snapping and snarling as they fought over the scraps, they fell upon their share snuffing, snatching and gnawing vigorously. A servant, unnerved by the chaos, broke the bottle from which she was pouring *kerare* to the poor. She was so stupefied by the incident that her legs shook under her, squelching the mud as she crouched on her haunches, and she kept rolling her head, not even daring to look at the broken pottery.

'It's the custom hereabouts to drop food or spill drink on one's clothes,' the beggar in the woman's overcoat was saying, pointing to the *kerare* stains on his coat. His companions started to mock him in whispers, then jeer aloud.

The peasant's dog had kept on whimpering throughout, but scarcely had someone tied him up than he dropped asleep. Nearby, a cow, bored to tears, lay on her side in the dung-heap, switching her tail and chewing.

The people in the hovel were still flinging whatever they did not want into the compound, thus affording the passers-by an opportunity to regale all their senses with the garbage: the scent of damp grass, the stench of spilt blood and incipient decay and manure – the flies swarming in dense clouds over it all. It was as though a thin jet of hot jellied sweat were creeping towards you.

Some Galla girls, horrified by the sun-warmed filth pouring on to them, held their noses and rubbed them with goat-droppings from their small gourds, with which their ancestors used to recognize a member of another tribe in the dark. They even spat and rubbed their feet about on the ground as though to rub out the spittle of this existence.

The people from the towns looked as if they were not expected to lavish their feelings on such people or scenes.

One by one, the beggars started to accumulate again. The hostess saw that she couldn't feed the newcomers. Purposely, perhaps, she disturbed the bee-hive, and as the bees buzzed around their heads and necks and started to sting them, the people fled. Even the dogs, with tails tucked between their flanks, bolted whining in every direction.

5 Woynitu

The sudden flight of partridge from the cluster of bushes at my feet startles me. I stop to watch the big bird rise up on its whirring wings to go over and down beyond the hills. I see the mass of living green where the sun beams down from the sky to make the yellow flowers whiter, and where the wind stirs the hot smelly weeds and *koso* flowers. I see the bees flying from one yellow cluster to another and cowering and bending them like drops of rain. I see the working bees flying to and from the beehives. I touch the tender green leaves on the trees. I smell the *koso* and *wanza* flowers. I hear the buzzing of the bees and the chirruping of the birds on almost every tree . . .

I see a beautiful red bird sitting on a bough whistling. Soon I see the mate flying from a neighbouring tree with a straw in her bill and start building her nest on the branch. A husband and wife, perhaps. Then I see a rainbow-winged butterfly on the near-by *besanna* flower. I brush its wings with my fingers trying to catch it. It flies away before I grab it. And I find myself pursuing it. It flies a little further and alights on a branch. And sits there drinking the sun-warmed water. I hate to startle it again and I simply look. A large fellow it is.

I sit on a gnarled root in a *besanna's* shade. I see the beauty in the yellow-white clusters of the *koso* flowers. I feel the smell of the earth under me – songs of birds, humming of bees, smell of *koso* blossoms, blowing of the wind – I feel that it is a place to be awake. I straighten my body and breathe the clean air into my lungs and I try to whistle a tune like the wind playing in the leaves above me. And I walk up a narrow path that leads under a thicket of trees. I go down on my knees, bending my head to miss the thorns above, and moving slowly under the bushes, and I crawl out into an open space. And I stand to brush the dirt from my hands and knees. And what do I see? The beautiful Galla girls passing a gourd of milk from mouth to mouth in the shade of a tree . . . Something like hunger and thirst rises in me. I want to laugh with them. To associate with them. And to drink from that gourd with them . . . And I walk towards their spot only to find they run away from me as though I am some kind of ghost . . .

Unhappily I sit down where they have been sitting. Some time passes. The rolling note of the ibis is heard nearby. And suddenly I detect a movement in a bush in front of me. A big movement as if it were a marabou that is hiding there. Slowly and slowly, I walk towards the bush. I peep through it. In a little clearance, I see a broad-shouldered man with large hands trying to kindle a fire . . .

Part Five

1 Goytom

The hubbub over a piece of bread and the preaching at the church, the landlady, the piquant little lady and the beggars at the *das* and the air filled with dazzling, dancing heat waves, I was simply burning and breathless. I wanted very much to splash some cold water on my head, and walked slowly down the lake.

At the edge of the water, a maiden was standing – with her face towards the lake. And as I was approaching, I took her to be the little lady I had seen on my way up the hills, in the church, and at the *das*. I saluted her from afar and got near enough to start a conversation. She turned immediately and walked away – without even showing me her face . . . wearing a long white dress fitting close over the hips . . . avoiding me like that. . . . And her smile, with a gold tooth shining in her mouth. . . .

The breath of *koso* and other flowers, and the air from the water carrying with it its peculiar scent, set my heart fluttering, longing for some venture – to follow her . . . burning or not burning, this sun . . . I see her pass behind a bush on one of the hills . . . sweating and breathing heavily, I walk faster and faster to reach it and not to lose sight of her. . . .

I listen to the sound all around, not with my ears, but from within outwards – subject to her before I understood her meaning. . . . And then, suddenly, I hear a voice. I hear a quiet voice, like the breath which suddenly blows through a dense growth of trees – quiet and yet emitting sad sounds – weeping?

I go closer and sit beside her, not looking at her and letting her weep as much as she wants.

In the sky, motionless, hang the hawks, with wings outspread, and eyes riveted intently on the grass. A fragrance like that of ambergris wafts like smoke across the whole mountain. The air is filled with the notes of different birds. I lie flat on my stomach in the grass beside her and start watching crickets and teasing them with a little twig.

Then, suddenly, without my knowing why, I sit up and put my

arm around her shoulders. I wonder why she doesn't object to it. Breaking a little prune shoot to pieces, she simply goes on weeping, her chin on her breast and her eyes low. I feel extremely attached to her. And I think that she nudges my elbow with her own. The next thing I know is that she is seized with a fresh burst of tears, and that I embrace her tenderly. She does nothing all the while, except that once she raises both her hands to tie her head-gear properly. An ox is striking wildly at the ground with its hoofs and horns, throwing cascades of earth and stones in all directions.

And the peasant! He must have been sitting all the while and looking at us – with no decency at all to turn away his eyes. And the boldness he is showing – trying to signal to me her beauty in his own person, by distending his nose, screwing up his eyes, and twisting his mouth to one side, as though hunting for civet.

I look at the girl beside me, her glance is now, direct, untamed, grave and questioning:

'So you like *koso*? I like *koso* very much. It cleans all kinds of worms from your stomach. . . .' I hear her saying, 'There are plenty of *koso* trees around here and all in bloom. . . . I like *koso* flowers too.' She folds her hands in her lap and looks into the distance with a fixed, immobile gaze. An obstructed light seems to glimmer somewhere in the depth of her eyes, painfully eloquent of a lovely soul. I feel as though dazed by a blow. I would never have thought that my body could bear such agitation. A draught of wind seizes her and wraps her thin skirt about her ankles, seeming to chill her.

'Have you seen a man flogged?' she starts again.

'Flogged?!'

'Yes, when they flog a man in the market place.'

'No, I haven't. My father has seen many though.'

'I have seen one.'

'You have?'

'Yes, my father.'

'Your father, I'm sorry.'

'Oh, nothing to be sorry about. He was flogged for insulting the governor of our province.'

'He insulted the governor and was flogged?'

'Oh, no, they said that he insulted the Emperor in insulting the governor.'

'And you saw that?'

'Yes, my mother and I and my brother too.'

'Where are your parents now?'

'My brother jumped into a river and killed himself soon after . . .
I like a river when it is full and overflowing its banks – roaring
down, carrying away cattle, huts and haystacks – I like it very
much. . . .'

'You shouldn't have gone to the market in the first place.'

'It was my brother's idea.'

'And you stood and watched while your father. . . .'

'They stripped him bare and put him face downwards on the
ground . . . Oh, I still see the swish of the *jiraf* in the air, the howl
of pain and despair of my father, his bare back swelling up and
covered with white and dark strips, the blood oozing and squirting
and forming patches, drops and trickles running down to the ground
– I saw all that.'

'And all that. . . .'

'Do you like watching blood spill?'

'No, I don't.'

'Why not?'

'I don't like spilling blood.'

'I like spilling blood – I like red – I like a big red fire – such as a
hut burning and the roof cracking in the middle and forming a
huge brazier; I like also forest fire – a conflagration; I like red
moon, red lamp, red soil, red pepper, red flower, red dress, red
curtain – I like red very much.' I make her rise and we walk slowly
on and on and I look at the girl again. Her face has already changed
to a laughing face – warm, with parted lips, her glance holding
a question no longer, only a light-hearted challenge.

'Do you like the colour of those huts? I like them – round and
plastered with clay and finely-chopped straw. I like especially the
damp yellow look they have on them. . . . I like millet also – I like
its smell when the underground storage pits are opened – damp,
mildewy and yellow.'

'But that's dangerous; it has poison called carbon monoxide.'

'What does it do to me?'

'Well, it will kill you.'

'It hasn't killed me.'

'It will, if it gets you in large quantity.'

'How will it get me in large quantity?'

'Nooo! no, I don't think it's good for your health.'

'We dry it before we grind it into flour.'

'Yes, that's how they usually do it.'

'The damp millet is bad, they say.'

'Yes, it is.'

'But I didn't hear them say that it will kill.'

'Well, you see . . .'

'I like millet when it is damp anyway. I like it mildewy. I like it yellow.'

'I came here with my father, you see, he's old and very ill.'

'Your father? You must be very lucky.'

'You didn't tell me what happened to your father after the incident.'

'After the flogging? Well, he was detained in prison for about three months and they released him.'

'Then he must be in good health and be working now.'

'I don't know. We have never seen him or heard of him after that.'

'Probably he has taken to the hills.'

'Who knows, perhaps he may be living in some forest as an outlaw.'

'I wish he had taken to the hills too.'

'Who had taken to the hills?'

'My father.'

'But why? Your father was not flogged.'

'No, he is flogging me instead.'

'Flogging you? I wish my father was here and flogged me.'

'Oh, you don't understand.'

'Then make me understand.'

'He doesn't care for me, you see. He simply wants me to serve him like a slave. And I don't want to do that. I want to serve myself. I want him off my back.'

'So, why don't you leave him and go on your way?'

'I can't; he's sick.'

'Well, you can go after he has recovered from his illness.'

'But he won't.'

'How do you know?'

'I know because he has some kind of incurable heart disease.'

'But he can still be cured by Abbo.'

'I don't know.'

'I like molten wax. I have brought fifteen wax tapers for Abbo. I made them myself by dipping a pile of muslin in a cauldron of molten wax. And then, I hung the soaked cloth up to dry . . . I like a yellow and gold border and fringe to wear on the head . . . I like freesias – I like yellow freesias, don't you? I like them very much.'

'I don't know even why I am saying all this.'

'Why? Because you wanted to talk with me.'

'But why should I tell you my personal problem?'

'You are afraid he may die?'

'May die?!'

'Perhaps, you don't want him old and suffering.'

'After all, he likes my mother's money.'

'I like old things and yellow things and red things and I like you. . . .'

'You, you like me?'

'I like your old father. I like old millet . . . do you know we haven't sown anything since my father left? All the bundles of millet hung by him on the ceiling of our house are still there – all laden with soot. . . .'

'All laden with soot!'

'My mother says, it will be good for sowing. If it is mildewy, it's not good, you see.'

'My father is mildewy . . .'

'Your father is mildewy . . . mildewy?'

Tall grass and grass flowers seem to close in around us concealing us, even from the hawks. White tufts of light gleam through the gathering clouds, and the coolest of little breezes caresses the cheek. I try to put my arm again on her shoulders, urged to embrace her. But instead I stop short. Tears start to gather in her eyes – tempestuous expanse of water – distinct – vague – she rushes headlong – topples over – I don't try to stop her. . . . I feel an uneasy dread which makes my legs tremble – sparkling with fire, the swampy mirror of water – I am looking at it through the interstices between the reed and sedge.

Standing at the edge of the lake.

2 The Peasant

He had already heard the good tidings from his wife and was contemplating it over the fire he was building:

'How handsome, I will be carrying a spear in one hand and a gun slung over my shoulders by a strap. . . .'

And Woynitu peeping at him through the bush was thinking, 'The huge pat of butter on his head melting in the sun, running over his hair, down the neck, over the forehead and all over his face – he looks no end of a swell, this peasant. I wish I could help him make the fire. . . .' Cautiously, she walked towards him and threw down by his side the bunch of sticks that she had picked on her way.

'How handsome I will be carrying a gun over my shoulder? I mean it. I will look really handsome,' he continued, seeing her approaching.

'You have a gun then? Let me make the fire for you.'

He tore a bit of kindling from a dry log, arranged the chips on a piece of dried cow-dung which was already smoking, and started to blow it until his face was strewn with ashes and cinders. The sticks began to blacken, twist, crack and emit jets of grey smoke until the whole mass raised myriads of sparks and broke into a fierce, red, roaring blaze. 'With my gun slung over my shoulder, I will be somebody here about whom the ladies from the town will have to think twice before they try to order him like their servant.'

'In this scorching sun, what do you want the fire for?'

'I hope your man will be true to his word. Otherwise, my woman will call the devils on him again.'

'Wouldn't you perhaps want me to roast the corn for you in the fire?'

'And no flint-lock either. A good breech-loader – that is what he promised my woman.'

'Haven't you heard the saying that there is no such thing as a beggar's choosing?'

'Yes, I have heard my wife saying it plenty of times.'

'Then, you don't have to be fastidious about things that are given to you free.'

'A breech-loader or the devils on him – it's your man that has to make the choice.'

'Butter helps to soften the skins of the head and face and prevent them from blistering during such a hot season, doesn't it?'

'If two of the devils are on him now, my woman will call three more and make them five at my making the slightest suggestion to her.'

'The butter is melting down into your eyes. It will make them smart if you don't watch out.'

'And don't I know when to make suggestions to her? She will say yes to anything I ask of her.'

Smiling, 'I don't think you'll be as cruel as all that.'

'No woman with a gold tooth can fool me either.' He untied his bundle, took out the flayed skin, and stretched it in the sun by nicking small holes round its edge and driving little pointed pegs through them into the ground.

'It looks very much like our sacrificial sheep, doesn't it?'

'You forget I'm a conjure-ploughman. You think I don't know my business. You think that it's my woman only who can save your man. . . .'

'Why do you say, your man? Don't you know he is my father?'

'You don't know that I have my little connections with the devils.'

'He is my father, you see.'

'And don't they know how to pay when they are served well – half of the meat for me to eat and the skin for my son to sleep on.'

'Don't tell me you've met them and they shared the meat with you.'

'Why do I have to meet them? Half of the sheep disappears into their stomach and the other half disappears in mine – that is, I take it and eat it.'

'How do you know that it is not some beast who has eaten the other half?'

'Beast or no beast, those who have eaten the meat must have the devils in them. And my woman has told me so. At least that is what she said the Book of God says.' Blinking at the fire, sneezing, giving a lurch and once in a while putting up his hand to screen his eyes and lolling at the fireside, he added, 'The devils live mostly in the air, water, and in dung heaps. And some live in animals and human beings.'

'And those who live in animals come and share the meat with you.'

'Oh, they could be from any one of the places.' He tried to settle himself comfortably at the fireside. 'And don't think that I can't go home now and rest there. I am no more of a shadow on your man than the priest.'

'Your wife and the priest seem to be intimate.'

'Oh, no, not proper intimacy – if you are implying that.'

'My God! Where have you gone to? I wasn't at all implying that.'

'And can't I chuck him out by the scruff of his neck if I want to?'

'Please, don't misunderstand me; I was simply saying they help one another.'

'They help one another, eh? And me, painting my body black and running around our hut doing all sorts of dances and throwing stones and all that during the night . . . you say I am not helping?'

'You mean you play the role of the devil?'

'No, I didn't say such a thing. I simply create the atmosphere for them. And then they come. And then my wife talks to them.'

'Have you seen any one of them at all?'

'What should I want to see them for?'

'Are they invisible?'

'You don't want to be a conjure-woman, do you?'

'No, I don't!'

'No woman with a gold tooth can fool me then.'

'I am sorry you misunderstood me.'

'Telling me I am not helping my woman!'

'Why do you put words in my mouth?'

'And don't I play my role well?'

'I didn't mean to undermine your role, believe me.

'Just because I don't have horns and a tail.'

'My God, you are much like them without that!'

'Gnashing of teeth and snorting and farting and all that . . . you think I don't do all those things. . . .'

'I didn't think so.'

'You think my eyes don't spit fire!'

'Please!'

'You think I can't munch and munch you until there is nothing of you but powder.'

'Please. . . .'

'I like you more when you are frightened – yes, you are more mouth-filling.' He sat up, untied his bundle again, took some *zelzel* of meat, and arranging them at the end of a stick, started roasting them on the embers of the fire. 'Would you like to taste some of these *zelzel*?'

'No, thank you, I'd rather have some of your corn, if you don't mind.'

'Sure, you can have some of the corn.' He had already eaten a great many *zelzel* before he started to speak again, 'It's a habit with me to eat a great deal when I am angry.'

'Angry? Angry because of me? I hope I haven't intruded on your privacy.'

'Ayeeeye! how delicious it is – much like drinking honey with butter.'

'You enjoy your meat, don't you?'

'I enjoy everything I do. I enjoy working and I enjoy eating.'

'Do you also enjoy pushing people around?'

'I like that very much especially when it is women.'

'But that is not manly. It means you are a coward.'

'Manly? Not manly? Me, not manly?'

'Would you perhaps want me to bring you some water in your gourd. I could use some myself.'

'I think you are calling for it.' His face, dark and angular like the peel of a boiled potato, assumed a resentful frown, and blinking his eyes he continued, 'Calling for it. . . .'

'Calling for what?!'

'For the devil in me – that's what.'

'For the devil in you?!'

'That lad of yours, he is a clever man and a fool. He doesn't like me, I know. But at least he should have tried to understand that I wouldn't turn up my nose even at a five-cents piece, let alone a five-dollar bill . . . and my woman cognizant of each and every species of proverb, anathema, and every species of proverb . . . if I allow her to do it all free of charge, what will become of me? Medallions and title only.'

The air was filled with the odours of roasted meat, of the sheep-skin baking in the sun, of damp and rotting wood, and the dying fire.

'The butter on your head is mixed with *ades* scent – it has a good smell....'

'My other woman likes it.'

'You have another woman besides your wife?'

'Why, this one has two cows and is always ready to put some butter on my head.'

'How is it that she has more than you have?'

'Oi, oi, she has more than that. Her husband is the clerk of the district. One of those young men from the towns – with lots of stories on the tip of his tongue but not the kind of lady's man I am.'

'And if he happens to catch you with her?'

'Lots of times, we have met in his house. He calls me his body-guard. He likes me.'

'He knows about the affair and he likes you?'

'He knows that I am a conjure-ploughman.'

'What has that got to do with your visiting his wife?'

'He is afraid of me.'

'What about your wife – is she not a greater conjure-woman?'

'She used to be the concubine of one of the poor Fitawraries of our district. She left him and married me.'

'Why did she leave him?'

'He got poorer and poorer every year.'

'And she left him and married you?'

'He has even cancelled this year, the annual feast he used to give on Abbo's anniversary.'

'The Fitawrary, you mean?'

'Yes, he couldn't afford it.'

'And you are not afraid of any competition.?'

'She doesn't care for him any more.'

'And now you have her, you don't care for her feelings.'

'I like her the way I like a woman.'

'You are the devil himself – in the process of changing, perhaps – you are not a human being at all.'

'My wife also thinks that way. But she likes me all the same. "I like you when the devil in you is showing," she says, "I like you when you look at me as if you want to swallow me," she says. "But I don't like you when you are angry," she says. It means providing me with a lot of food because of it, you see. She doesn't like that. She likes me only when I want to swallow her.'

'You are a rude and boorish person.'

'My woman calls me a lout. She doesn't like my stomach – when I gormandize the food she puts before me. But she likes me all the same.'

'She is right. You are a real lout. All the louts put together can't come near even to half of you.'

'This morning when I was holding your hand, I felt like wanting to swallow you too.'

'Oho! you felt that, did you? You felt like wanting to swallow me!'

'And I wasn't hungry, with that five-dollar bill in my breast pocket. I was satisfied and I wanted something to complete my happiness.'

'And you got that happiness?'

'No, I was only holding your hand.'

'What was the kind of happiness you wanted?'

'I wanted to feel like when I eat a fat spayed sheep.'

'The kind of happiness you get from eating meat?'

'Sort of.'

'What is the feel of that kind of happiness?'

'Well, you feel big.'

'But you are big.'

'You feel ten times bigger than you are.'

'But you are always the same, aren't you?'

'No, I am always bigger in front of my meat. It's like I have killed a lot of men.'

'You are perhaps sometimes crazy.'

'It's like becoming a Fitawrary all at once – with land and medallions.'

'You are simply crazy.'

'It's like being the high priest of Abbo.'

'You have a snout instead of a face.'

'Like being a governor of a big province – with lots of people bowing and bringing spayed sheep and goat and calf and *teff* and . . .'

He blinked at the sunshine, sneezed and gave a lurch. And then putting his hand to screen his eyes, looked around. He yawned as if his hunger was beginning to be acute again. A cool breeze blew from the lake. Patches of cloud softened the harshness of the sun in the blue sky. And the embers of the fire subsided into a soft glow under the ash. He yawned again, covered his mouth with both hands – desperately trying to control a mortal anguish that was seizing him, a whirlwind of frantic intoxication. His eyes bulging despite the smarting, he lifted both his hands from his mouth and with a heavy movement, coiled into a heap, flashed his scales dimly, and applying his favourite stranglehold, took her by the hand and turned her roughly towards him, clasping her delicate body in his embrace.

She was momentarily stupefied with terror. Then she felt something snap like a green stick and pain ripple through her body. And she gave a piercing scream – struggling – gnashing her teeth terribly, sniffing heavily – and sobbing. . . .

He picked up his bundle and without even giving her another look, left her beside the skin of the spayed sheep and scampered down to the lake, mumbling to himself, 'How tight she is! It's not often that a man meets such a woman. . . .'

His happiness was consummated.

3 *Woynitu*

Men and women chattering and chirping near by and life seething and bubbling as if nothing has happened. What could that conjure-woman be doing now? And what became of her performance of witchcraft over fire and over water? Why don't the herbs with precious qualities which she claims she gathers, help her to get rid of this lout of a husband? Should she not really be now howling and beating her breast, cursing the day of her birth and all her ill-fated life with a human offal like him? And for a man like that, she does all the housework – chopping the firewood, fetching the water, feeding his child and his insatiable appetite and sewing a patch on to his trousers - to a husband that does such a shameful thing to her. . . .

And me sitting here all the while, what should I do? With my blood still trickling. I feel nauseated. I wish I could throw out once and for all. I wish I could vomit all the filth he has put into me . . . Oh, Jesus Christ! How am I going to walk with such a pain in my stomach? How am I going to face people with shame written all over my face? I wish I could throw out everything. And this *netela* of mine – how am I going to account for it, with blood-stains all over it? I suppose I should try to scratch some parts of my leg – make a big wound, with lots of blood flowing all over it. Yes, that's the best way out. Goytom will never suspect .Nobody will ever know about what has happened to me. Not even the conjure-woman.

Oh, Jesus Christ! Here he comes back again, walking towards me as if he has done nothing and trying to show that wooden smile of his. And how puffed-up he looks, as if he has conquered the whole world. I hope he won't try to talk to me. I hope he won't try to help me. . . . And how he is looking at his sheep-skin. Smiling and feeling pleased about it also. He is pulling out the pegs from the ground. And what could he be mixing? Clotted milk and linseed flour, perhaps. He is smearing and spreading it on the skin. What a man he is. He makes me feel like the skin. As if he is smearing me with that mixture. He is folding it up, fur outside, and trampling it. To make it soft and smooth. What a man! I don't really know what I feel towards him. With that scent of salt and sweat in him. With that butter. If Satan were here, such would be the acrid stench of his armpits. And the fright he has pitched into me: he makes me feel like a tiny bird in his clutch. . . . What could be the right sort of feeling for me to have towards him? Abhor him, detest him, want to kill him, perhaps? And the way he spits the tobacco juice in his mouth all over the place!

'It has good skin – this spayed sheep.'

Oh, no! I'm not going to talk to him. I feel like throwing up. I think it's coming up finally. . . .

'I will tread it underfoot for a considerable time every morning until it becomes soft.'

Yes, it's starting. It's coming up. I feel the bile in my throat. I should perhaps try it with my finger. . . .

'Every morning, I will tread it and put it away covered with fresh grass. I'll put heavy stones on it to press it down and prevent it from drying.'

It has started to come up – a bit at a time. And my intestines seem to be struggling to come out. . . .

'Then, I'll clean the fur and peel off the skin, leaving it as soft as . . . as . . . as your body . . . and I will give it to you as a present from me . . . Oh, oh, you are vomiting. Let me support you from the breast.'

Please. . . .

'Aggg! I feel like vomiting too.'

Not here, please. And don't crush me.

'Half of my *zelzel* has come out.'

Wooy! yellow liquid – pure bile. . . .

'It has some corn in it too.'

'Leave me alone, please. . . .'

'Now, drink some water and wash out your mouth.'

'You wash out yours.'

'And give me your *netela* – I'll wash it for you at the lake.'

'No, I will wash it myself. . . .'

'That lad of yours is by the lake. You don't want him to see you in it, do you?'

He is there, isn't he?

'How beautiful that blood looks on your *netela* – bright-red like the blood of a chicken – bright-red.'

'You look as though you want to swallow the *netela* too. . . .

'If I had my own *netela*, I would have given it to you and kept this one.'

'Why do you want to keep it? It's not good for people to look at it. . . .'

'I don't care for people. I like it. I like looking at it – bright-red like that of a chicken's.'

'All right, take it and wash it and come back as soon as you can. . .'

What a man! He still has a bit of heart in him. Vomiting with me as he did and wanting to help me. . . . I can't say what I feel about him. . . . Why not call Goytom and make this boor suffer the consequences? I don't know why really. I simply can't do it. And what do I feel then? I feel nothing. I feel empty. I wish I could douse myself with cold water or take a nap to collect myself. . . .

'It's all cleaned at last. There's no trace of the blood on it any more.'

You have come back at last.

'It took me some time to locate some *indod* to wash out the blood.'

You have cleaned it well.

'I'm sorry I couldn't keep the *netela* with the blood on it.'

'And keeping it if your wife chanced to see it?'

'I don't care any more – conjure-woman or no conjure-woman. I don't care . . . she is not like you.'

What do you mean not like me?!

'You are tight and mouth-filling.'

'Please don't talk about that. . . .'

'We are going to do it again after three days.'

'You are mad. . . .'

'Yes, I'm mad about you. I am anxious to do it on the third day.'

'Even if you attempt to come as near as touching me again, I'll claw out your eyes. . . .'

'It wouldn't hurt you as much as it did today.'

Don't make me mad!!

'I wish I could bring all the three days backwards.'

'What human offal you are . . . you . . . you . . .'

Part Six

1 Goytom

My father and his often-repeated story of the young man whom he had sentenced to be flogged, Woynitu with her gold tooth shining in her mouth, and the pretty little lady in the white dress – I couldn't understand why they should start to haunt me during the day-time. What could be the meaning of it all? Haunting me during the day-time. I wanted very much to find out more about the lady. And since I had nothing else to do in the next hour or two, I came towards the *das*.

All around the *das* everything was quiet. Even the priests seemed to have left. What was still there was the rubbish that lay entangled and jumbled up in heaps – rotting and exhaling a suffocating smell. I entered the *das*.

Whatever food remained from the priests and guests had been collected on one of the low-legged wicker tables, and the children of the neighbourhood had gathered around it with their knees drawn up to their chins, waiting for one of the deacons of the church to finish reciting the usual prayer over it.

'We pray that God accept this feast to the poor that is given in His name. . . .'

'Amen!'

'We pray that He forgive the trespasses of the deceased.'

'Amen!'

'That He grant him a place with Abraham and Isaac.'

'Amen!'

'And we pray that God grant the wife of the deceased strength and comfort in her sorrow and loneliness.'

'Amen!'

'That He bestow on her the blessing of health, wealth and happiness.'

'Amen!'

'And let us pray the Lord's Prayer together—'Our Father which art in Heaven

Hallowed be thy name

Thy kingdom come. . . .'

To see them wolf the remains of that food was to hate eating.

Soon after, a hubbub arose in the *das* – the meal was over. The children were collecting the drinking utensils and the wicker tables to return them to the store of the church. Each one of them carried some article and left the *das*. And returning afterwards, started to tear down the *das* and to shout and run madly about in the ruin.

'Let us play soldiers,' suggested one of them.

'Yes, let us play soldiers!' shouted the rest and ran towards their respective homes.

Some armed themselves with sham swords made of wood, some with reed guns and lances, some with shields of wickerwork made of rushes and some with hand grenades of *emboi* and mud. They all returned prepared.

Then one party was chosen against another and the battle started. Now charging in a compact mass, then changing the order and following each other in a string, then halting and confronting each other again – they were shouting, gesticulating, skirmishing, spearing, shielding, retreating to the fortress in the courtyard, sliding from the stepping-stones across the stinking mire and emerging filthy; throwing dung and rubbish on those who were chasing; then changing tactics, one party hiding in the bush and the other going out to find them, fighting, fighting, fighting until they were exhausted and out of breath . . . and then the victor and the defeated, all dishevelled, dirty and bleeding, no different from the dung heaps which surrounded them, turned to the burial of the dead.

They placed them on litters and carried them in procession to Abbo. Some of the boys dressed up as priests, and the remainder of the troop followed as mourners, wailing and violently rubbing their foreheads and faces with the borders of their garments. They made seven halts on the way up, at each of them burning the sham incense over the bodies, and the mock priests each reading a psalm or two until all the hundred and fifty-one of them were allotted. Then extracts from a mock holy book were read at the church, and the dead were decently buried.

And after they had gone through it all – patriotism, respect for the dead, mercy for the prisoners of war, triumph for the victors – I could imagine what the welcome feast at each home would be like:

soiled, dirty, and haggard-looking as they were, their welcome would be whips, slaps, kicks. . . .

Medallions and titles!

The little lady wasn't there.

2 *Woynitu*

She felt a terrible sound in her ears. Terrible because it was human and yet without words. The sound rose to a roar that deafened her. A sudden nausea rose to her throat and subsided. Her buttocks seemed weighted with lead, and she walked slowly and lingered against trees and the cold bushes by the way. It was as if she had touched the solid bottom of despair. With no further chasm below. For some time, she pondered on why she did not take her rest here, upon the bottom of utmost humiliation, and end it all. But she went onward with the terrible pain between her thighs. Her ankles scratched and baked with mud and her legs trembling and shaky, she seemed not to notice where she was going. Now and again, she lost her way in the thick masses of horse-weeds, ragweeds and bushes.

The sun had started to sink behind the ragged line of trees in the distance and the sky had paled. The twilight was languid and low purple clouds lay over the horizon. The earth, the trees, the hovels had started to darken slowly. At intervals, mild lightning quivered in the air.

It was as if she were the only person on the mountain. She stopped suddenly. With the wild sounds hushed, the silence sent out ripples of fear throughout her body. She thought of Goytom. She wondered what he would say if she told him what had happened to her or if he would still love her the way he used to. 'I have become one with my mother, after all,' dreamily she spoke aloud to herself. It was soothing to hear her own voice. She opened her mouth to hear it again, but nothing came out of it. And she didn't especially care about what she was doing any longer. She picked a little bunch of grass blades, twisted them and threw them away. And although the place was getting darker, she sat down again. She began hitting her thighs with her fists. She pounded the same muscles with all her strength. But she couldn't feel this hard enough. She picked a sharp rock from under a bush. And she began scraping up and down on the same spot until her hand was bloody. With the fiery hurt in her thighs and her hand, a sodden heaviness weighed down upon all her limbs. Her pulse started to beat faster and her throat to become tight. And with the wind coming through the branches and rustling her hair and the bottom of her dress, her eyes burned. She felt as though she was sinking down slowly into the dark ground. She couldn't control herself and started to weep.

A while later, she fell back to the ground. A warmth was spreading through her. It seemed that she was sinking down into a place warm, red and full of comfort. She let herself lie limp on the wet grass, and after a while, her dizziness lessened and her breath came slow and easy again. A deep and holy sadness took possession of her. And she sat up holding her head between her hands, Then she saw the gold cross dangling from her neck – the present from her father.

The sky had blackened. And all the stars were covered with thin cloud. The air turned chilly. She got up and went down to the lakeside – straining to catch another human sound above the beating of her heart.

3 The Little Lady

Now he opens and takes out the stomach of my spayed goat, and his disciple-attendant carries it on to the clean grass to shake the contents out and peel off the tripe. I can't understand this preacher. With his hair like that! Newly plaited and matted. Why was he so hesitant to talk about my friend and the memorial feast she had given? I don't understand why. I think, perhaps, I shouldn't have come to him. Am I not in a way degrading myself? The father-confessors in the town usually come to our houses, and when we go to their houses it must be for some special reason: when we are deeply agitated and need their help urgently. And we go either early in the morning or during the evening. I don't know. I haven't perhaps come at the right time. Even so, he should try to be hospitable to me. His manner as it is is unbecoming of a man of God. And the way he heard my confession, sitting with his back towards me by my side. 'Now, I'm ready for the confession,' he said. And how I tried to tell him politely and humbly, 'Oh my God, I am deeply and heartily sorry for having offended thee, I don't know how the devil got into me. On the day my friend's husband died (What a friend he was to me! Even his wife used to be jealous of us), I was so disturbed, so agitated. I didn't know what I was doing. The devil must have followed me from the funeral ground. To have felt what I had felt that day. It was hot and I was weeping. I didn't know what I was doing. I wanted somebody to comfort me, to be by my side. I wanted somebody terribly. . . .'

'Let us not dwell on pettiness, please,' he cut in – rude and not priest-like at all. His disciple-attendant was smiling to me from afar and I thought he was urging me to go on. I knew at least that he understood my problems. I could see him with his fingers playing on his lips, and smiling to me. I felt encouraged and asked the preacher, 'Is it a mortal sin or a minor one?'

And I heard him say, 'You haven't told me yet.'

After all the things I was trying to explain to him, he said I hadn't told him. A preacher and a big one at that. I knew I had no right to argue with him, 'I haven't told you, have I?' I said. I was irritated and angry with him in my heart of hearts, but still, I had to go on with my confession, 'Well, as I was saying, it was hot and I was weeping. I wanted somebody terribly. Somebody to whom I could confide what I felt. To unbosom myself, to weep on his shoulders and chest. It was hard on me, everything. The lamentation, the funeral rites, the way my friend's relatives wailed. I couldn't stand it. I wept all day. My tears refused to come. His relatives kept looking at me. I tried hard for my tears to flow. But there were no more tears. How much I wanted a pinch of red pepper to put into my eyes. Even when I thought of my saliva and tried to apply some, I saw that it dried on my face immediately after application. I wanted somebody by my side. Somebody that I trusted. . . .'

'The hard facts, please.'

I pretended not to have heard him and continued, 'The devil was in me, I think. I was so frightened, so empty, so lonely, I wanted somebody. Somebody who would embrace me ... protect me ... I wanted to fall off my bed.'

'Fall off your bed ?!'

'Yes, it was terrible, but I wanted that all the same.'

'When was it you said you felt like that ?'

'The day my friend's husband died – after the funeral.'

'You wanted somebody to make love to you before your friend's eyes had shrivelled and his hands had withered ?'

'I felt it at the burial place.'

'You couldn't suppress your feelings ?'

'I couldn't. I wanted somebody to hold me in his arms.'

'And you got that somebody ?'

'No, I didn't.'

'Then, what did you do ?'

'I controlled myself for the day and during the night I wanted to leave the mourners and go to my home.'

'Why did you want to go to your home ? Wouldn't it be defying accepted custom not to commiserate with your friend, for at least a night, in her great sorrow ?'

'It would be, but I wanted to call somebody that I knew.'

'Somebody who had improper intimacy with you ?'

'No, we hadn't gone that far.'

'Did you overcome the temptation finally ?'

'No matter how hard I tried I couldn't make it.'

'And you went to your home ?'

'No, I couldn't make it.'

'Thank God, you still had your guardian angel by your side.'

'Then it's not a mortal sin, is it ?'

'It's mortal all right without that.'

'Oh my God, what should I do ?'

'As you know the priests around here are poor people. Tomorrow is Abbo's anniversary. They are going to pass the whole night in the church. Some are lay-readers, some are incense burners, some are caste prayers silently reading religious books, and some are singers and drummers – all are dedicated men who have given their life to the service of Abbo. They need your help.'

'I will see what I can do,' I said.

'You have fat spayed goats on your farm here,' he said.

'But the sheep are fatter,' I told him.

'The sheep is a holy animal. Even Jesus Christ Our Lord is called the Lamb of the World. I don't have a heart to kill a sheep,' he said.

And I see now why he wanted me to bring him a goat rather than a sheep. All that piece about Jesus Christ was simply talk. He certainly knows what he knows. What an incision he has made from the tail to the hind hocks. And how he brings out the two hind legs through the opening – all the skin stripped off in one piece. He is now cutting off the forelegs at the knees. A clever fellow – the three legs tied and one seam from the tail to the hock sewn up, and with the head cut off, and the neck used to fill in– he is preparing it for a grain container. A clever fellow. I can see now the meaning of the Lamb.

'Would you like to taste some of these pieces of tripe?'

'No, thank you, I don't usually eat raw tripe meat.' The disciple-attendant expects me to eat raw tripe cleaned and wiped on the grass. He doesn't even take the trouble to wash it. Who does he think I am after all? Some peasant woman from the countryside? And this preacher with all his pride! True I sinned when my friend died a year ago. But I have ever since kept my cleanliness. And am I not happy the way I am. I don't even wish to get married. I have plenty of money and land. I have my own house to live in and other houses to rent. What should I want a man for? What a preacher! He certainly looks a man of the world despite all his plaited hair and costume. And he knows what he is doing too. But then since he is the chief preacher around here, he should have come to the memorial feast. And evading my questions about my lady friend. I think I should have told my confession to some other priest. It shouldn't have been him. . . .

'I was wondering why you have come back to see me. Busy as I am, I haven't had time to talk with you.' He comes towards me drying his wet hands on his trousers.

'I thought perhaps you might have time enough to lave me in holy water.'

Oh, my God, what have I said? I come for one thing and say another. Why don't I ask him the reason for his evading of my questions about my lady friend?

'Do you wish me to read all the holy books over the water or only the psalms?'

'Is there any difference?'

'Yes, a great deal.'

'Then you know what's best.'

'Would you perhaps prefer the holy water to be sprinkled on your head to washing in it?'

'No, I'd rather wash in it.'

Wash in it? What am I saying? In this cold water? I must be crazy to say such things. The devil must be putting words in my mouth.

'That means, I will have to use the cross every time I pour the water on you.'

'You mean you dip the cross in the water every time?'

'No, I mean holding the cross with my left hand on your body and pouring the bowl of water through it with my right. If you wish my student to do it for you, it will, of course, be cheaper.'

'If I am not inconveniencing you. . . .'

'All right, I will do it myself then."

I don't know why I am saying all this. Why couldn't I tell him what I came for? Why should I want to wash in the holy water with all the readings and everything? Haven't I paid enough for my sins with my spayed goat? And how am I to stand the cross touching my body? And the sun going down and the cold evening approaching.

'You prepare the meat for the priests until I am through with the lady. Oh, wait a minute. Before that, check if there is sufficient water in the house and prepare it for me in a basin,' he instructs his disciple.

Why shouldn't I postpone it until the morning? It's getting colder and colder now. I think, before I go into his house, I should tell him I have changed my mind . . . Oh God. . . .

'We'd better go in then and start. I don't wish to be late for the evening service at the church.'

I follow him . . . I follow him . . . I don't say anything. I hope to God there isn't sufficient water in the house. Then the young man will have to go up to the lake and fetch it. He may be late. I will suggest then that we do it in the morning. Yes, that's better. I know I can't stand the cold water . . . and the cross touching my body. . . .

'You have sufficient water in there?'

The young man has gone into the adjacent room of the house. He hasn't answered yet. I hope there isn't. . . .

'You can see it yourself.' He comes with a big basin of water, 'If we need more, I can bring it.'

'I think we can do with what we have. You go on with your other work.'

No escape from it . . . what should I do? Oh my God, save me from this cold water . . . save me from your cross. I'm weak and frail. I can't stand cold water. . . .

'You sit here until I finish the reading.'

And I sit here without doing anything. I simply sit goggle-eyed – not saying what I came for. Waiting for the cold water and that silver cross. It will make me shrivel. . . .

The touch of it.

4 *Goytom*

Things come back to you on this mountain top – the white clouds settled over the far-off mountain and the deep valleys; the thin ribbon enveloping the mountain from bottom to top and lifting skyward in white shreds of mist – it is a pleasure indeed to watch all the paths and hills of this valley. It's as if you are on an island in the sea of clouds. And here at the ridge, the light thin air is clear. You can look over the sea of rolling white clouds all the way to Addis. The tops of the dark hills jut up like little islands. The wind above you is filled with streamers of mist rising from the wild flowers, trees and bushes. And you, breathing it into your lungs. Listening to the singing of birds and the blowing of the wind. Listening to the pilgrims murmuring . . .

How beautiful it would be to pass your life observing the wild life of bees, birds and animals that live around you. Watching the rugged land, the wild flowers, the rock cliffs, the air and the skies. Plenty of time to live and think. How good a world it is to grow up in. Growing your corn, potatoes and cabbages. Growing pumpkins of all kinds – pumpkins with long necks and small bodies; pumpkins as big around as the bottom of an earthen pot; pumpkins and more pumpkins – white, yellow, green and brown . . . It would be heaven, indeed, to live here – hunting for wild bees in trees; hunting for wild animals; and growing your own garden with all kinds of cabbages. Living like a hermit. Living a life as free as the wind. With every weed, flower, and tree on this mountain put before you. You can use the blossom, the bark and roots for medicinal purposes. You will have remedies for everything including ignorance. If only you could have the proper mixtures . . .

Sad, you can't drive automobiles over these hills. There aren't even loose gravel roads. Only cow paths, goat paths, rabbit paths and footpaths. I don't really know when we are going to build real roads – down by the deep valleys and around the rocky-walled hills and over the mountains.

Oh, if only everybody knew what we have and what we lack! If only we re-examine our life instead of taking it on faith. If only we could teach these meek and worshipful peasants. If I can tell it all to them . . . But who is going to listen or understand? Talk about the social situation in your country, you are thrown out of school; talk out your miserable working conditions and you are fired from your jobs; speak up about certain injustices in the government, and you land in gaol; talk at all, and you are left without even your friends. Why, I haven't even succeeded in making my own father understand me. Quite a gentleman, I am. But an oddling . . .

And me a young man. An educated young man . . . Oh, yes, at least I have learnt to spit into a gaudy handkerchief. To use fork and knife. To knot my ties and put on my shoes. An educated man – an oddling by any standard . . . And I'm supposed to save Ethiopia . . . Save her from whom? From myself, I guess? By prayers of mourning; by indolence and strong drink; by the pleasures of the body; by submission and humbleness, and by ignorance . . . Yes, I'm going to save Ethiopia. No, not by work; not by pride in what I have; not by dignity as a human being; not by becoming hard and strong; not by building strength for our real true purpose of building a nation. No, these are not for me. They are for those wandering out into the darkness beyond tomorrow . . . Let me just sit still and learn to knot my ties; to use my fork and knife; to blow my nose into a handkerchief . . .

Yes, I'm the greatest of oddlings. Before filth I hold my nose with my fingers. Before injustice I hold my peace. What is it to me that these people live in hovels built with far less attention to needs than fences for animals. For animals are more valuable in this country than men. At least we have started to export some . . .

Yes! Yes! I sacrifice the things in hand for the good of the hypothetical whole. I believe in the tongue instead of the fist. And how I shout! We must start from the practical bottom and work up! Not from the theoretical top and tumble down. The old traditions must be smashed! New ones must be created! We must forge a whole new pattern for Ethiopia! Must have faith in the human soul. Must-must-must! Rot and contradictions. Fiddlesticks!

As if I am wearing blinkers all the time so that I won't see sideways or into the future. As if the armour against oppression here is not patience. As if people are not forced to be unjust in order to survive . . .

Oh, yes, things come back to you on this mountain – with the sun dropping down in the west and with this strange light between bright day and dark over the white mountain. With the sounds of shepherds driving their animals home to the pasture. And with all the superfluous creatures around you, you feel sort of eerie, like the sun dropping down into oblivion. You feel gloomy and moody. And all the feelings I have against Fitawrary drop down with it . . .

I can imagine him now in that hut. Propped on his wooden pillow and staring upwards into the soot. I'm sure all he can think of is his illness, or perhaps his work – going out every day to collect rents from his houses . . .

5 *The Supper*

The usual contributions of the devout of the parish – *injera*, white and black, two types of *wot* stew, bread, raw meat, and about ten very large jars of beer – were collected at the house of the preacher and ready for supper. The priests and scribes had collected together again. And they sat at table according to their rank and started drinking and eating at intervals. When they were through, they cleaned their fingers elegantly with the black *injera*. They stood up, and the preacher started on their behalf to praise the villagers and the little lady for their contributions. He spoke especially of the lady – about her generosity, her virtue and her reward that would be Heaven. He even likened her at one point to Mary Magdalene, and thanked her, in conclusion, most of all for the spayed goat she had sent them.

The remaining food on the wicker-table was then left for the deacons and the lower *debteras*, who entered the hut soon after and sat as never anybody had sat before. And when they had finished, imitating and copying the ways of their superiors, they cleaned their fingers with whatever remained, drank two or three gourds of beer, and left. Then, the remainder on the table was gathered into three big baskets and was given to the beggars.

Some of the priests, it was true, had difficulty in retaining what they had eaten and drunk, and had to bend down once or twice on the edge of a small stagnant pool – a pool which sounded from time to time as if it had come alive under a sudden downpour. In the dry season, it was sometimes used for drinking water.

The beggars, therefore, were given very little either of food or drink. And yet since whatever they had was something over which the word of God had been said, they were satisfied and passed the time as merrily as they could. Many times, one or another of them had gone out of his way to support the chest of some who seemed unable to bend over the edge of the pool.

The majority of the priests, however, had done very well despite the enormous quantity of food and drink they had consumed, and the hangover that would probably catch up with them by the morning.

Then there was a discussion about the annual lunch due to be given on the morrow by the now poor Fitawrary of the area which had been unexpectedly cancelled, which gave rise to a vague premonition of the *Tabot* punishing them all. After this they went up to the church and started the usual sequence of prayer, singing, and holy dancing.

Part Seven

1 *Goytom*

The short shower of rain had stopped. And once more, the coolness of the night had set in. The warm aromatic scent of the *koso* and *wanza* trees, dried up by the day's heat, mingled with the sharp freshness of the wet earth round the marshy banks of the lake. Deeper and deeper grew the shadow of the night over the mountain, colder and colder the air, until the twilight caused the slopes to soften in outline and the bushes and rocks to seem too small and merge with the blackness. The dim light of the new moon had risen to a pale half circle of light against the dark blue of the starry sky. And standing up on the horizon against the hills, the graceful trees seemed taller and more dense. Lights had begun to shine from the bonfires all over the place. And the mystery of the evening – the croaking of the frogs, the chirping of glow-worms, the rasping and whistling and whirring of other insects – had started to seethe and bubble with life. Now and then, a gust of wind rustled over the hills and came down to the edge of the lake, making the bonfires blaze up in showers of sparks and sending out ruddy splashes of light over the people sitting around them. Then, a gentle breeze followed, dulling and glowing the embers of the fire, casting a smaller, wavering light on to the faces – now fading away, now shining clear again like hope unreplenished.

All the water was calm, and not a sound occurred to break the stillness ashore. The conversation of the devotees, dampened by the shadow of dusk, had resolved itself into a single sound which resembled the humming of bees – every word therein seemed disconnected, but in each such sound there was something gently sad, softly prayer-like.

About one hundred yards away from where I was, two tents were pitched. One belonged to a rich merchant and the other to the peasant's landlady, who I was told used to be a minister's wife. The rest of us camped under the cover of the trees.

Seated with Woynitu and the servants, I started to stir our bonfire with a bit of charred stick. Sparks of gold began to fly, joining the midges gliding to and fro over the blaze. Now and then, night moths subsided into the flames with a plop. They writhed, cracked, and were changed into lumps of black. Now and then, the flames picked out our servants, yawning, limping and blinking their sleepy eyes. And now and then, they picked out Woynitu lying stretched beside me, her face thrust upwards and her hands clasped behind her head. She stared dumbly at the zenith, where a few stars were shining and the moon was beginning to weave a soft, liquescent scene.

A little farther away, near the golden radiance of a bonfire, the sick maiden that I had seen by the lake was playing with mud. She saw me as I was looking at her, laughed a little, stood up, laughed again and came towards me playing with the lumps of mud and singing a song:

'It rains
very heavily
and the mud
Oh what a delight
it would be
to patch a wall
with this soft
wet earth.
It rains
very heavily,
and the donkey can't move.
The driver beats her,
the poor beast,
methodically, slowly and
slowly
piece by piece, she falls down –
To have seen it.'

At the end of it, she seemed to be waiting for approbation, and a storm of applause broke from the surrounding bonfires. One of the men yelled at the top of his voice and the audience screeched and bellowed long after the song was ended. The maiden kept chuckling through her teeth, seeming to choke with laughter. Then just as unexpectedly, she started to weep, quietly at first, and then her weeping rose to a terrified hysterical sob. Looking at those tears flowing from motionless eyes, you thought her demented, feeling at the same time an irresistible impulse to comfort her. You saw in her youthful freshness a slightly sleepy face, a kind of enchanted carelessness. I saw myself in her, as if I had known her all my life.

The babel of voices ignited by the maiden's song continued to hum all around. Somebody's humour triggered off laughter. Every few moments a voice was heard saying, 'Yes, I enjoy women ... I enjoy drinks. ...' And listening to them talk like that, you would imagine that they were happy. Broken and worn out as they were by the struggle for bread, they talked jestingly and humourously with careless audacity of expression, with dare-devilry and flattering encomiums on their various talents.

One of them was relating a story of his cousin; 'And was there any ignominy he hadn't to endure for eating the governor's bread? Until one evening his wife came to his rescue...' he was saying.

'How was that?' another man egged him on.

'She told him that she had rather go stick in hand and beg for alms than yield to the master's request.'

'You mean the governor forced his servant's wife to sleep with him?'

'Yes, I mean that all right.'

'He must have been a fool not to advise his wife to fulfil the master's will.'

'What?!'

'Yes! Even men of rank send their wives and children to their superiors.'

'You must be crazy to talk like that.'

'Why do you say that? Don't we have here in Ethiopia some tribes who willingly favour you with one of their wives when you stay with them as their guest?'

'I was talking about a man who had only a wife, not many wives.'

'I really don't see the difference – one or many.'

'Do you know what some foreign communities in our towns are doing to satisfy the top officials?' someone else cut in.

'No, I don't. You tell us.'

'They send their children and wives to the officials.'

'Their children and wives ?!'

'Yes, by consoling them that they would wash themselves clean when they return.'

'What would they get out of it all ?'

'Well, I hear some of them haven't paid the state taxes for twenty or thirty years.'

'You are talking horror.'

'Horror or no horror I am telling you of the actual practice.'

'What if we hear about that gentleman's cousin?' some soft-spoken person put in, not wanting, it seemed, to hear about the foreign communities.

'Yes, go on, please! Tell us what happened after the wife brought the news.'

'Well, he cleared out that very night and started to live as an outlaw.'

'How many people did you say he has killed until now ?'

'Nine men! And he has robbed most of the spayed sheep and goats of the surrounding villages.'

'And he hasn't been captured even once ?'

'Oh, he was captured twice. But fortunately, he managed both times to escape from the police station. They say Gabriel is his rescuing Saint.'

'I admire his pluck.'

'I shall go on wiping out my score with the governor, he says.'

'I, for one, pity such a man,' said the soft-spoken person.

'He would kill you if he heard you say that. Pity! Those who have had the opportunity of knowing him are proud of him. They envy him. Pity ?!'

'Hasn't he lost the treasures of holy humility, humble faith, tenderness and love ?' continued the quiet voice.

'Those treasures are for cowards not for real men of courage. They are qualities of the dead not of the living.'

'Do not cast your pearls before swine, says the Book. That's why you do not agree with me.'

'Watch out old man! I'm not the type to be bullied like that.'

'Life has caught you with the alluring bait of poison coated with honey.'

'Please!'

'And you are tormented by the throes of despair.'

'My person cannot bear such insults any longer.'

'Your person? Don't make me laugh.'

'Don't drive wedges into my heart.'

'Go on hiding your soul under your heap of rags. You will see who is the worse for it.'

'Don't open the abyss before me.'

'You shouldn't be ashamed of your external rags and dirty hands but rather of the internal ones.'

'Don't blind me by lightning.'

'Bursting with envy you go on talking about killing poor people or defaming some foreign communities. About whom you know nothing. Except tukul gossip.'

'Don't blind me by lightning!'

'You and your cousin and some of these people who seem to be enjoying your story are all pitiable creatures.'

'Pitiable creatures?!' He rose up and hit the old man on the head. And the old man, raising his shoulders, supported his head with his hands for a moment and fell face downwards. 'That will serve you well!'

'He should have known what blood is trickling in your veins,' spoke one of the admirers.

'He should, shouldn't he?' Standing astraddle the fallen man for a short while, he saw that he was unconscious and returned to his seat.

The night got darker and darker, the air blew in a gust for an instant and a soft chill haze breathed down from the sky – and the fallen man pricked up his ears, 'I never expected you would be like your cousin.'

'Expect it then from now on.'

'Their hands and feet stained with henna, and their eyelids with antimony, our women nowadays are indeed beautiful,' the lover of women and drink began to speak again. 'Once I had a neighbour whose wife I coveted. One day when he was at his work, I entered his house wearing a leopard skin and holding a spear with my right hand, growling and roaring like a wild bear. . . .'

'Please, we do not want to hear about your show of endurance in words,' cut in the killer's cousin. 'We have seen a lot of pretences – striking themselves with fire, pretending to cut their shoulders with swords and all that sort of nonsense. What we need nowadays is real men – men like my cousin.'

'Does one have to capture a phallic trophy by killing a man to be accepted as a real man?' The one who was knocked down started speaking again.

'If not that, at least he has to take revenge on his enemies – not preach that kind of nonsense of yours.' He spread out his arms and flexed his muscles for all to see. 'Even if it is women you are after, like that man over there. You have to go out to tear the pitchers of water down from their backs and rend their dresses and sleep with them when you meet them at the pond – at least I know that is what they understand.'

'Every thought is like dough, it's worthwhile to knead it well.'

'Dough?! That's work for you and your kind – the lick-spittle – not for the real men.'

'You will be pleased to see me get in a rage and lose my temper, won't you? It's a source of amusement to you.'

'Yes, I want to prove if your trousers are worn by a man.'

'According to you, to prove my manliness, I have to fight. And to see that justice is done to me, it's your wish that I go out and rob strangers, like your cousin, so as to bring the ruler into disrepute.'

'You have got my message, but I don't think you can practise it. You are frail and weak like a woman.'

'Don't you think that the days are gone by when men had to do such things as you are saying?'

'No, they aren't gone by – they're in fact at hand.'

'May I ask what you're doing here at Abbo, if you are the type that practises what you are preaching?'

'I have my own kind of request to make to Abbo. Life is tit for tat. If he helps with what I am embarking upon soon, I'm going to bring him a bull.'

'And what if he doesn't?'

'Well, I'll have nothing to give him. I may even be forced to change to another patron saint – to St Gabriel, for instance. I'm told he helps people with my faith and conviction.'

'I hope to God that all your plans will not be a rainy day's dreams.'

'Hope for yourself. And besides, it's not for you to see what the future has in store for me.'

'You know as well as I do that grass stops growing if a stone falls upon it, and worms begin to breed under the rock.'

'Yes, I know – when a stone like you falls upon the grass.'

Very strange people, talking like that they went on through the night. They didn't even think of going to sleep. And hearing them I was overwhelmed with melancholy – a sense of instability – and yet at the same time with an energy and a vibrating urge to survive. I stretched myself beside Woynitu and continued to inhale the resinous odour of the firewood.

The half-moon had already sunk behind the near horizon of black mountains, visible on the right, and shed a faint tremulous twilight on their peaks, in sharp contrast to the impenetrable darkness wrapped about their base. Once in a while, the light from our fire put Woynitu's face into relief. At one point, a bad dream woke her up, and finding there was nothing wrong, she looked at me sulkily, turned over and went to sleep again. A languid, sluggish damp, cold wind started to blow.

And I went on drowsing amid the thick, rasping voices around me.

2 The Ladies

At the tents was a group of people from the towns – well groomed and business-like men with smart wives; fat-necked boors with big bellies, flabby flesh and puffy cheeks; and sophisticated back-street women. They were kicking up their heels, sitting or lying on their backs around their bonfires, guzzling and gossiping.

The little lady especially was having a good time. With the landlady, she had started the usual gossip about their friends – a recreation which helped to develop their intellects, sharpen their powers of observation and make them feel superior to those around them: to those around who listened wonderingly to their speech, nudging each other whenever anything struck them.

'That's the problem about the educated man,' the pretty lady was saying.

'He had risen from the mire to consort with princes and generals.'

'How truly said.'

'And how soon he forgot that he had climbed the ladder of success because of his wife – my aunt's daughter.'

'What did you do finally when he refused your request?'

'I rang his superior and told him about it, of course.'

'And I'm certain you got your man released from prison.'

'Could you imagine it? He was supposed to have killed a competitor of his in the mercantile business.'

'A competitor?'

'And how the witnesses lied. . . .'

'What did they say?'

'They witnessed against him saying that they had seen my friend shoot five bullets into the stomach of the deceased.'

'And it was all a lie?'

'You don't think it was true, do you?'

'I've heard so many versions of the incident I don't know which one to believe any longer.'

'Three of them are now serving time for two years.'

'For falsifying the truth?'

'That's right. And two of them ran to the countryside and are being hunted still.'

'But tell me truly, is it not a fact that your friend killed the man?'

'He might have killed him, but not with five bullets.'

'How long have you known your man? He must be quite cruel.'

'Cruel?! No, he's not cruel. He's just like any other man when his interest is in question.'

'You must love him to have done so much for him.'

'If only I could give him a son or a daughter. . . .'

'Why don't you marry him?'

'Am I getting old, my dear? I really sometimes wonder why he doesn't propose to me.'

'Perhaps he is afraid of you.'

'Why? because of my late husband being a minister?'

'He may be from a humble family.'

'But didn't I help my husband to be what he was? He was also of a humble origin, you know.'

'Yes, I know.'

'If only Abbo accepts my offering and gives us a son.'

'It's getting very cold. . . .'

The stars had faded. The dark sky paled behind a covering of soft fleecy clouds. A grey mist rose from the ground. And the fire slowly died down until there was only a fiery patch, barely sufficient to render visible the shadows of the near-by rocks, while the area around emerged spangled with sparks of glow-worms.

The night, purified by the cool air, lulled the drowsy ear.

'I wonder what these goggle-eyed peasants feel in watching us and listening to us like this,' the big lady commented, her plump ruddy face shining with complacency, noisily smacking her lips for the wretched beings.

'I doubt if they ever feel anything, except, of course, hunger and thirst.'

'Do you think they know what they are missing in life?'

'No, I don't think so. . . . Perhaps, that's why they are watching us like this – amazed at all the things that they can do without.'

'Crippled creatures. . . .,' the big lady recapitulated and, rising up to enter her tent, walked straight up to them as if they weren't in her path at all. The little lady gave them a wide berth, mounted a mule that was dragged to her, and went up to her lodging. And the servants curling their lips contemptuously followed their mistresses.

And the poor people feasted their eyes upon them.

3 The Conjure-woman

Rushes with a slightly aromatic odour, fresh grass, wild thyme and mint were strewn upon the floor during the day-time. And fleas hidden in their hollow stalks were coming out in tactical units now. A coffee pot and a small portable charcoal stove were placed at the left side of the conjure-woman. And at her right, twelve demitasse cups on a wooden tray. At the door and two other places, incense was burning, strewn over some glowing charcoals placed on pieces of broken earthen pot. A mixture of roasted corn, wheat and beans was scattered inside and outside the door for the spirit of the house and the mire. A skin of python hung outside on the top part of the door.

Long after midnight, the conjure-woman, seated on a high stool near Fitawrary, was at the height of her meditation. She was listening in terror to the sounds which her *qat*-stuffed imagination seemed to conjure up beyond the walls, and was talking in a hollow distant voice.

'The unnameables are pursuing and enmeshing her with fears and anguish,' the priest was interpreting to the Fitawrary.

'Do you think the devils will keep their appointment and appear to-day?' Fitawrary asked.

'Don't call them devils, please. They will be offended . . . they are called the unnameables.'

'Offended?!'

'I hope they will not take it to heart. And clutch firmly at the branch she gave you and never look up in case they appear. . . . And never laugh if you happen to hear some seemingly unnatural noise – I mean even if you hear them fart while dancing.'

'The branch is supposed to protect me from their anger?'

'Yes, hold fast to it.'

The cold night breeze came stealing through the open door and with it the scent of the dewy grass, of *koso* flowers and dung from the yard. And the conjure-woman, her manner more apparent than the matter, went on calling the various devils by name.

'I'm having a sinking feeling that comes on when one has just had a near escape, and thunder strikes a near-by tree,' commented Fitawrary, craning his head and pricking up his ears trying to distinguish everything that was taking place near him.

A shower of stone and mud had started to clatter on the hut from outside and it looked as if it would never stop. And the conjure-woman, growling and whining like a wild beast, striking herself with a staff ornamented with rings and brass, seemed as if she would never recover from her lethargic state. A peculiar atmosphere, baneful, blighting, shrouded the hut like an invisible cloud. Again and again, fresh gusts of agitated feeling caught up with her. She tried to bring out laughter like that of a bleating of a goat, until finally, with bleary eyes, tousled hair and a hideous smile, she mumbled, 'You're suffering from a painful palpitation of the heart,' and fell down from her stool.

'So, the unnameables are not responsive to her call tonight . . .' started the priest again.

'What could be the reason? Could it be that they are offended as you have said?'

'It could be that or perhaps they may not have been given all they require for their appearance . . . I don't know, perhaps, they might need a small black sheep or something.'

'And what shall we do now about her?'

'Oh, she will wake up in due time.'

'It's very strange.'

'On the night of Abbo, the unnameables fly far away into the mountains. It's very difficult to entice them here.'

'You mean they are afraid of Abbo?'

'Yes, as long as the name of God and his angels is echoing in the heart of the pilgrims and in the air, they have to keep themselves as far as possible.'

'I hope we will be able to entice them by tomorrow.'

'It's like bombs and bullets whirring and exploding in the air.'

'What's like bombs and bullets?'

'The name of God and his angels.'

Outside, the peasant, painted black all over, and covering only his inexpressibles with leaves of *besanna*, was hiding and gliding in the bushes.

In the distant countryside was seen the glare of conflagration – at one place, the flames spread tranquilly over the sky and at another, having encountered some bush on fire, they burst in a whirlwind and hissed upwards to the very stars.

Part Eight

1 *The Awakening*

Goytom

Already, the heavens had begun to grow coldly grey. It was the early dawn when the completeness of the silence attunes the soul to special sensibility, when the stars seem to be hanging strangely close to earth, and when the air breathes chilly, and men cuddle themselves up and sleep soundest.

From the top of the mountain, pure, clear, distinct as if bathed in the freshness of the moment, came the sounds of the church bell: first, only single sounds, then coming faster and faster until they floated and stayed on the air for a while. And then, after a moment of silence, the last series of trembling notes, one stroke after another, echoing themselves through the purple dawn like some kind of sad booming sigh.

The pilgrims woke up; and yelling, shouting, and plopping their feet through the mud, sometimes falling, they headed for the lake.

And then, slowly, the cold grey mist started shifting. The landscape became visible under the greyish-white sky upon which the pale dim stars were hardly visible. The red glow of dawn began gleaming in the East. The horizon began to grow clearer and more blue. A fresh, penetrating breeze sprang from the Awash valley in the south, and a shimmering mist rose like steam over the earth and water. The leaves began to stir softly. A faint morning breeze passed wanderingly over the earth – from thicket to thicket, from copse to copse. On the bushes, heavy and bent with their loads of dew, and on the great bowl of water, shining out under its breaking mist, the dawning day threw up its purple rays and slowly poured forth floods of fresh and resplendent light. A stirring, an awakening, a breathing full of joy and hope – all living nature burst into voice and song – grasshoppers, crickets, and thousands of other insects filling the air with their shrill, incessant sounds.

Faint streaks of light began to reach heavenward. Red wisps of cloud drifted above the rim of the lake. A raven flapped across the face of the flushed and glowing sun. The night chill relaxed and a genial warmth penetrated forest, hills and huts. The day had begun.

Each man and woman, before bending to reach the water at the lake, pulled a handful of grass and cast it upon the water, then washed hands and face and headed up to the church.

And our hearts filled with the bitterish fresh scents, the delicious coolness of the morning, the mists enveloping the whole lower landscape and most of the far-off mountains, and the loud and resolute songs of the priests – a mixture of a sob, a laugh, and a cry of dread, which sounded like a moan, desperately trying to break into a melody. So we entered the churchyard.

The district chief came along after us on his trotting mule. Stirrup leather of bullock skin. Crupper and girth of bullock skin. Bridle and headstall of twisted hide. The red saddle cloth flapping in the wind. Trappings jingling with metal pendant and bells. A young man trotting at the right side of the master's mule. A gun in bright satin case over his shoulder. Another man trotting in front of the master's mule, crying, 'Out of the way! Out of the way!' The master dismounted in the churchyard. A red cover was immediately thrown over the animal, reaching from the ears to the fetlocks. A protective measure against the evil eye. I followed the master with my eyes. And his mule too. He looked at all of us for a moment as if we were specks of dust in the yard. His loose drawers extended to just under the knee, where they fitted tight, and were gathered round his waist by a thong or a belt. A loose shirt over it, and an embroidered damask on top of that. And over the damask, a fur tippet. And on his head, a hat made of straw and grass. And in his hand a white horse tail with a wood handle.

And why shouldn't I? I went closer to the church wall as he did. And like him, I started to pray. He was district chief with his own fertile land. With streams swiftly flowing through it. With natural pastures of long grass interspersed with flowering shrubs. Herds of horned cattle and droves of horses and mules. His own abyss – maze of peaks, ridges, canyons, cliffs and rock spires. I prayed like he prayed. A district chief. He has his scribe with a raw-hide case containing pen and ink. His cottage. Even his own villa in the towns. Half a day's journey on a mule takes him to some cold, windswept plateau. Half a day's journey to some hot countryside with nearly tropical heat. Half a day's journey to a mild climate. Tropical, subtropical and cold climate in the hollow of his hand. I prayed. I prayed hard. Some four or five concubines and fancy women, perhaps. Not a man of pot and *tej* houses any more. The bar, the big hotels, the gin-palaces, the saloons are where he meets his friends. A lucky man born during the battle of Adowa or during one of the famines or one of the Little Rains. And I born in the month of May 1950. He is a lucky man. A man who served his country in one of the street courts of the good old days. You simply hailed your man before one of them. The Judge passed his sentence immediately. Debtor and creditor linked to each other with jingling chains. To prevent the escape of the debtor. To discourage the creditor from Shylock practices. The good old days. The chain never removed until the debt was paid. The pair remaining in bonds for months – eating, sleeping, and performing all the routines together.

The good old days. He fought in one of those great battles. Bullets flying through the air from the muzzle of his gun to the enemies' bodies. The enemies' bullets suspended in mid-air. St George or St Abbo hovering over his head and protecting him from the streak of destruction. The good old days. He never had to carry his ration of food to battle. He and his escorts went to one of the near-by peasant huts and took whatever they wanted. Even if they happened to fancy the wife. The good old days. He has still in his bedroom his silver shields. His swords with gold and silver decorations. His guns and rifles of many patterns. Old flint-lock. Breech-loader. Mauser. Menesher. Alben. And pistols.

I prayed. I prayed hard. I prayed fervently.

The rock and tree squirrels climbing up and down the roof of the church. The wild pigeons roosting in the grove. The pledges of sheep and goats baa-ing at a corner.

The service went on as usual. A deacon had started to read the gospel aloud. And when it was over, the bell began ringing for Kyrie Eleison, Credo, Tersanctus, Agnus Dei and the Benediction of the Blessed Sacrament.

The pilgrims had started to cower in the doorways of the church, gazing inside with a calmly enigmatic gaze. I wanted very much to go into the church. But it was not possible with all the jostling and pushing. I stood by the church and started to pray. Now and then, a face with features sharp or coarse was thrown into relief by the flickers of the wretched wick tapers. Now and then, someone struck a match and lit a wax candle stump. Every crack and crevice and every nook and cranny was covered with blurred light. Poor church. It doesn't have ceilings dripping with chandeliers and thick carpets in which you sink to your ankles, like the Trinity Cathedral in Addis. Stumps of wax tapers were lit again, one near the lay reader and the other near the altar. Someone dropped a pinch of incense into the censer. And the religious song. One led off with a tune, resonantly, in a pure voice. Some others chimed in with him swelling the chorus. And the same sound desperately trying to break into a melody soared far and wide.

Then Fitawrary was carried into the churchyard on his litter. Followed by the conjure-woman. He made the sign of the cross as soon as he was placed near the wall of the church. Woynitu brought him some fresh *immet* (incense ash) from the incense burner. He applied some of it on to his face, neck and chest. His eyelids opened wide, his arched eyebrows expressing withdrawal and astonishment. His face convulsed a little. A strange kind of rattling sound escaped from his throat. He then asked to be taken into the church for the Sacrament.

After the Sacrament, he was brought back again to his place by the wall. His face had assumed a strained expression. He looked as if he was trying to say something important. The failure to say it must have caused him inexpressible suffering. The district chief didn't seem to want to witness any more of it. He left for another spot in the yard. Then I saw a figure bending over Fitawrary. And I walked towards her. Her shoulders had a soft curve and her breasts a finer upward tilt. And when she raised her head to see me, the first rays of the sun sifted through a crack in the leaves of the trees fell upon her face. She must have been struggling to control her tears. I saw that Fitawrary was also looking at those eyes. His face had assumed a fatherly look. The girl looked as if she were frightened of the look. Strange girl. How she sang for us at the lake that mud and donkey song of hers! No doubt she has a big, big heart.

Fitawrary closed his eyes. And the girl left for some other place.

And then Woynitu walked to his side and took the girl's place. Gazing down into his face as the girl did. And Fitawrary applying his knuckles to his eyes tried to open them. Looking up at Woynitu in a bleary sort of way. Looking at her. And the next thing I saw was Fitawrary motioning Woynitu to him and embracing her. I even thought I saw some tears in his eyes. He must finally have realized that she was his daughter, after all. With all the odour wafting through the air. The odour from the yard. The odour from the dead fires. The odour from the damp forest. And the odour from the rotting wood of the church. They must have stirred up the quiet waters of his soul. Must have caused images to rise from depths which he had never before been aware of. Must have caused him to change his will. I felt something too, seeing him. I got nearer. He released Woynitu and his face assumed its usual stern and serious expression. Then, turning his face to the church wall, he sighed deeply, shuddered a little, stretched himself out, his chest heaving painfully, and tried to lie still. He kept on looking at the door with wide-open eyes. The conjure-woman ordered that he be taken back to the hut. And he agreed.

And Woynitu accompanied him.

2 *The Peasant and the* Ferenj

Goytom

The peasant walked around the church, gaily rubbing his hands together and grinning. He told the pilgrims that his wife could perform witch-craft over fire and over water and gather herbs with precious healing qualities. He even produced some flags, for those who cared to buy, which, he said, were among the herbs which the dragon in the lake was kind enough to let him pick from around his abode. An elderly woman approached him and asked, with tears in her eyes, if he had anything at all for her rheumatism. He was about to give her one of the flags when all of a sudden she changed her mind, left him, and headed for the church door. She prostrated herself before the door as soon as she reached it and started praying to all the saints, and all the ministering spirits and miracle workers. Calling them by name – Abba Gubba, Arbaetu Ensesa (The Four Animals), Hesanu Kirkos (Kirkos the Child), the least known of the holy martyrs. And then, 'Mother of God, Holy Virgin, Immaculate Mary!' she cried. She dipped her fingers in a corner of her *shemma*, murmured some prayer over it under her breath, touched her face and her breasts with the incense ash, and proceeded to do her genuflections, over and over again. A dirty ragged man, weighed down under his collected food and bending his head forward on his chest, stood at the church door hugging himself and trembling with fear as if in a shivering fit. Later, I saw the woman go into the church and come out of it, huddled up in her *shemma*, her eyes low, and the Sacrament inside her.

At the foot of the trees inside the yard, elderly men and women sat praying. At one tree, there was a man moaning and grunting with his hands clasped upon his knees, his head sunk upon his breast, and his face contorted as though something were stifling him.

Outside the fence, on a stretch of grass, the dancers were stamping round in a ring, shouting a religious song. At the refrain, the circle broke up, the dancers turned and faced each other in pairs, whirled round, then shouted the words of the chorus aloud and repeated the dance. The ecstatic ones danced apart, spinning, swaying or doing intricate syncopations with their feet and waists.

The peasant seemed to have been successful. He went around murmuring to himself a long and involved formula against the evil eye. He bragged that he had a love potion which was as sure in its effect as hellebore (used to kill lice), and almost as speedy. He said that he practised numerous crafts. That he could write on goat- or sheep-skin and on paper. That he could teach people to play on the *washint, kerar,* and *begena.* And that he could even teach anyone interested the ritual dances performed before the *tabot.*

A foreigner who had been following the peasant closely and was looking for an appropriate place to outsmart him, started, through an interpreter, to speak on the quality of the occult craft. First, he called on two of his students, led them to a tree, and pinioned them to it with his magic before they had time to realize what was happening to them. Then, he chose the peasant, took him to the edge of a cliff, and slowly pushed him down amid the outcry of the spectators. The peasant's knee gave way, he threw up his arms, turned a somersault, rolled down the slope and stopped, hanging on a ledge of rock. And from the spectators arose marvelling, and great swearing of oaths. The peasant was immediately and safely returned to our midst. The look of courage which showed in his face at the beginning had now vanished and had given its place to one of furious anger. He struck the *ferenj* in the face with the flat of his hand, tottered backwards about ten steps and fell among the bushes. I couldn't say which one was reality, the fall or the slap. Stamping his feet, clenching his fists and screaming with fury, he rose up from where he fell and went in the direction of his hut. The *ferenj* however continued his show, bending copper coins between his fingers as if they were so many sticks. You thought how the miraculous weakens the wills of men as much as fear.

An airplane passed very low, its noise reverberating near and far. Then the noise faded and the airplane disappeared.

In the land of thirteen months of sunshine.

3 *Woynitu*

Coming down from the church, I sit here waiting on my father. Wiping the streams of sweat from his face to keep them from stinging his eyes. Twisting my legs loosely about each other. And moving my eyes from one corner of the wall to the other.

The sick woman has already left. And as there is more space, it shouldn't be stuffy. But it is. The heat is suffocating us. I feel as tense as the deadly quiet before an explosion.

My father is feverish now. His head is trembling in his hands. And all his muscles are stiff with the effort to keep it still. I stand back by the wall. And he turns to look in my direction. But he doesn't seem to see me. He cleans his eyes again and again with his palms. A film seems to have settled over his eyeballs so that everything around him is blurred. I suppose I am one with the walls for him now.

I go to him and touch his hand. He holds it with one of his hands and closes his eyes. Then he lets my hand go and blows his nose with his fingers.

Looking at him, I feel as though I know him as well as I can know any person. I feel I am safe with him.

'Are you all right?' I ask him.

'Yes, yes! I'm all right,' he says.

I ask him if he wants anything.

'No, thank you,' he says. He holds my hand again of his own accord.

'Are you sure, you don't need anything?' I say.

'No, thank you,' he says again and releases my hand. I feel like unbosoming myself to him, and I say,

'That peasant . . .'

'Um!' he says.

'That peasant . . .' I say again.

'He thinks I'm a fool,' he says.

In the condition he is in, I should think it would be difficult to put the matter before him, I tell myself. He could become dangerous if he wanted to . . . I restrain myself.

'He thinks I'm a fool!' he says again. And I don't say anything more. I look at him . . . I look at him . . .

I walk out into the open – into the high sun of the afternoon sky, and I start to breathe the fresh air through my nose and open mouth listening to the ibis and expecting to see a marabou that might chance to fly over the mountain.

4 Goytom

At about noon, the priest who bore the *tabot* (the square canopy of the ark with the ten commandments) and the other priests, scribes and deacons who carried the other church paraphernalia, led the procession. And immediately following came a group of men each carrying a spear in one hand and an old gun slung over his shoulders by a strap; and then those that had only cartridge belts round their waists and over their shoulders – cartridge belts which gleamed with shells of many calibres, many of them empty brass cases, but still presenting a brave appearance to the rabble. Some of the belts had added to them a sword girt to the right side. And then came the horses and mules caparisoned with bright coloured saddle cloths, shining lances and jingling belts. And then, of course, bringing up the rear came the rabble – the main segment of the village. And they all proceeded down to the lake.

And arriving at the lake, the preacher blessed the water by raising his hand over it and the people started to bathe in it anew.

The chiefs and ladies and priests who thought it beneath them to go to the lake with the common people were sprinkled by the preacher.

And as usual, the great ceremony of regional dances and songs began to be performed. And at its conclusion, towards high noon, the parish and pilgrims, despite the reluctance of the priests, prepared to move back to the church.

Part Nine

1 The Revelation

Half-way up the hills, something happened to the procession. Something that they hadn't expected. The *tabot* stopped.

Word was passed from man to man to the effect that the *tabot*-bearer had refused to move, or rather the *tabot* had fixed him to the spot refusing to be carried farther. Great concern and anxiety was shown on every face. And a group was formed immediately to chant and pray for the bearer's release. In the meantime, at a respectful distance from the *tabot* and the perplexed rabble, the preacher was trotting and cantering in the smoothest manner possible. He was perhaps the only one who was not bewildered when he turned back and saw that the procession had actually stopped.

Nobody knew about what he had been before he came to this place some five years ago. Some said that he fell from grace, short of growing wings, and left his hermitage, owing to some love he had shown to a shepherdess. Others said that he had left his hermitage by the order of God, and that he would be called back anytime. And still others argued, the scribe in particular, that he was no spiritual man at all but a devil's son born of a woman – (it wasn't unusual for the devils to lie in wait at a pond and rape girls when they came down to fetch water – at least that was the conclusion one would draw from the numerous victims that were reported at the time.) Whatever the origin of the preacher might have been, it was at least popularly acknowledged that he was no ordinary mortal.

It was also said of him that he could travel on foot to any place the spirit might direct him (just as Abbo used to do when he was on earth), faster than he could by any vehicle. He was seen at one place one day, and at another place, some one or two hundred kilometres away, the next day. At least that was what the people said and there were many, especially truck drivers, who could vouch to this fact. How he did it, whether he actually walked all the distance or flew by developing instant invisible wings, nobody could say.

He never rode either a horse or a mule or a vehicle of any kind.

Or if he did, he was never seen. However, he himself was a horse. At least that was what he affected to be. On Abbo days especially, he trotted and cantered, sniffed and snorted. He even sometimes squealed. And sometimes, he acted like a horse affected with roaring. People said that he was under the influence of the horse in him. It was impossible either to talk to him or stop him, once the horse got control over him. And the few times he was free were perhaps the times when he was overcome by the Spirit of God or the Spirit of the body. When he was overcome by the Spirit of God, he preached; and when by the Spirit of the body, he sat at table and ate – bowing and submissive, as he called it, to the greatest king on earth, food.

And so when he saw that the *tabot* had stopped, he wasn't bewildered. He cantered and galloped to and fro in front of the procession, stopped unexpectedly, perched himself on a large and pretty *woiba* – wide-spreading and shady, with the bunch of purple-coloured flowers which contain a flat seed used by the priests to dye their garments yellow, hanging from each branchlet – and started slowly and modestly to preach on what brought about the impending doom.

Across from him, before a small, thorny bush, the conjure-woman was standing and seemed to be hesitating whether to stay there or not – the ground was covered with grass, the *wanẓa* trees and myrtle bushes were in full flower; and the wild, climbing, pink peas in festoons of bloom were hanging down from most of the trees. But the thorn plants were also in abundance – their thorns strewn all over the place.

The conjure-woman had always difficulty in walking through thorny bushes in her beautiful festive dress. She felt awkward. And, the thorns would either tear her dress or enter her bare feet, or both. And besides, they always caused her, or rather the idea of one of them entering the ball of her foot caused her, a moment's shiver throughout her body, and a sinking feeling of pain. She never could say whether she liked such moments or not.

'My children, my children, open your eyes! Look at what's happening before you – and look well! Look well before it is too late!' The words were coming from the *woiba*. The conjure-woman seemed to have decided at last to leave the spot, and made her way towards the preacher.

'Let not worldly grandeur rob you of your everlasting home in Heaven. Allow not the beauty of the cloth to cover and suffocate the beauty of the soul. No – never allow such things to happen to you,' the preacher was saying as he saw the conjure-woman approaching.

She was wearing a white cotton dress, made tight and elaborately decorated towards the wrist, the neck and the front, and wrapped tastefully round her waist to hang down to her feet. A *netela* – loose *shemma* – hung from her round shoulders. Her hair was gathered in tiny plaits over the whole surface of her head, the ends hanging down in ringlets over her neck. Coquettishly, she was playing with a pink kerchief – now covering her hair with it and now sliding it down to her neck. Round her neck, she wore a silver necklace, and alongside of it, a blue silk cord to which were attached a crucifix of silver and a few charms, including a specific one against barrenness and an amulet containing mysterious ingredients. And on her ankle she wore silver anklets.

The chant of:

'Protect us from impending danger

'Shelter us in Your forgiveness

'For Mary's sake, Your mother . . . ,' was heard from the pilgrims. And the preacher spoke louder and louder –

'Repent, repent, oh, ye sinners! The eighth millennium, the hour of reckoning, of repentance, of wailing and gnashing of teeth, of war, of terrors and destruction and of the coming of Jesus Christ in all his Glory – the Judgement Day is upon us. . . .'

The conjure-woman was standing close to his tree. And she was looking at him without obstruction and without in any way attracting attention.

'Kyrie eleison, Kyrie eleison

'Oh Christ, Oh Christ . . . ,' was echoing in the mountains. And the conjure-woman started to study the preacher intensely.

She had taken in his general appearance, his posture and physique at a glance, and she was looking now at his face, his powerful and commanding eyes, his prominent nose, and his determined forehead. And in the meantime, she was beginning to wonder how it was that such a man could still have a young-looking and charming face; and what he would look like if he washed away the red soil which covered his plaited hair and beard.

'Oh Our Lord, Oh Our Lord
Oh Christ, Oh Christ. . . .'
She pondered the fact that such a man could never have known a woman in his life.

'Repent! Repent! Oh, ye sinners. . . .' The words were coming out of the tree louder and louder. And the conjure-woman was now looking at a small framed picture of Jesus Christ beneath a transparent cloth, which a young deacon was carrying near her. She noticed especially the forehead, the nose, the lips and the straight and long hair which was lying on the shoulders. And suddenly as if struck by something, she turned to look at the preacher.

She saw a strange resemblance between the face of Jesus and that of the preacher.

'Oh Amlak (God) Oh Amlak
Oh Christ, Oh Christ. . . .'
Even the hair! If it were not matted, it could come down on his shoulders. She shook a little and made the sign of the cross three times and tried to tell herself that it was her eyes that fooled her. She looked again first at the picture and then at the preacher.

'Kyrie eleison, Kyrie eleison
'Oh Christ, Oh Christ. . . .'
The people were putting in the chorus all the energy left in their sweating bodies. The conjure-woman suddenly felt angry, she didn't know why, and walked away towards a near-by *wanza* tree which had large white trusses of flowers known for containing a lot of honey. A swarm of bees hummed away from a branch over her head. The tiny emerald and gold bee-eater could be seen levying toll on the passing insects. And the conjure-woman thought that she must have been angry because she had forgotten her status for a moment, and had mixed with the rabble around her. She promised herself to stay where she was now and read the Book of Psalms. She tried to tell herself that after all she had known the preacher for over four years and that he wasn't worth listening to. She took the book from her son and stood reading it.

It wasn't reading in the ordinary sense of the word though. She had never studied the alphabet and she never actually read. What she was doing was simply turning the pages of the sacred object, slowly and gently, turning them one after another while at the same time reciting some parts of the Psalms which she had studied by heart. She went on turning pages like that until she had finished reciting. She felt more like a conjure-woman that way.

'The eighth millennium, the Judgement Day is at hand. It has finally come upon us,' the preacher was saying, pointing at the *tabot* which still hadn't shown any movement.

'Oh Amlak, Oh Amlak

'Oh Christ, Oh Christ. . . .'

The conjure-woman's son attired in a piece of white cotton shirt stood behind her, carrying over her a sunshade of neatly plaited grass with his left hand, and brandishing a fresh *woiba* in his right hand. The green of the land and the white of the raiments contrasted vividly, and the whole scene – the long, streaked lights blending perfectly with the vertical shadows thrown by the trees – breathed a kind of soft beauty. A short distance away, the mules of the pilgrims were by turns currying with gentle teeth a beautiful black mare.

'Won't that be enough for a sign to show us how much we have transgressed the laws of our Lord – to show us how much we have trespassed His divine will?' He looked towards the conjure-woman and caught her eye just when she contracted her brows in a frown, crossed herself and was turning away from the mule scene. She was especially repulsed by the sores she saw on the withers, backs, bellies and sides of the animals. And by the fact that the owners hadn't brought the animals to her in time.

'Oh Egzyo (Lord) Oh Egzyo

'Oh Amlak, Oh Amlak. . . .'

And the action of the mules at such a solemn occasion! Why, after all, she never even drank water fetched on Sundays or coffee pounded on any of the Saint's days. And she fasted, besides the occasional ones ordered by her confessor as penance, at least two hundred of the two hundred and sixty days. And on top of all these, she exorcised the demons from sick people in the name of the Father, and of the Son, and of the Holy Ghost.

She stopped reciting her psalms and walked back with quick steps towards the preacher.

'Or do we still have to be warned by famine, plague, or war? Do we have to wait for some holocaust – some kind of unheard-of punishment?'

'Oh Amlak, Oh Amlak
'Oh Amlak, Oh Amlak. . . .'
The conjure-woman was now standing a few paces away from the preacher. She was perspiring. She noticed how profusely the preacher was sweating too. An almost irresistible desire spread in her heart – a desire for something cooling. She looked up again at the trickling sweat on the preacher's face and she wished that it were something else instead – melting butter, for instance. She fancied a huge cold pat of butter on the top of the preacher's thickly tressed, red-matted hair. She thought of waiting on him with a soft cotton cloth in her hand, rubbing away the melting butter in the sun.

'Oh Egzyo, Oh Egzyo
'Oh Egzyo, Oh Egzyo. . . .'
The butter was melting and running down over his head, over his hair down the neck, over the forehead, and she was softly and gently rubbing it off with the cotton cloth from circulating his ears and from entering his eyes. The mules had already started to squeal, swerve and jump to break their tethers.

'Oh, no, my children – no, no! Our people are not lacking in understanding. They know when the time has come. They know it by the slightest sign. And they know that they have sinned – and that all of us have sinned. . . .' He stretched his hand upwards into the air, lowered it slowly, and placed it on his head, only to make a short picking at his hair with his fingers and put his hand down immediately. . . . The conjure-woman still in her dream world took out one of her favourite silver-framed hair pickers, took the cotton cloth with her left hand and the hair picker with her right and began picking at his hair.

'Kyrie eleison, Kyrie eleison. . . .'
'Some of you give shelter to thieves and criminals instead of handing them over to the law. Sometimes, even those that betrayed their Emperor and country! Some of you listen with ready ears to vagabonds and vagrants who revile and defame your superiors, instead of reporting them immediately. You eat animals which have teeth in their upper jaw. . . .'

She was gently picking at his hair and carefully spreading the plaited hair.

147

'And animals that do not have cloven hoof. Some of you even eat bush pig and wart-hog, and now ...'

'Oh Egzyo, Oh Egzyo
Oh Amlak, Oh Amlak. ...'

She was still spreading the hair. Her shoulders were trembling a little. Her hands were hurrying.

'And now, you shout, "Oh Amlak, Oh Christ!" How come you forgot the eighth millennium is on you. The time when servants shall rise against their masters. Children against their parents. The time when children bite the hand that feeds them. Rising against their Emperor. Against the Emperor who feeds them with milk and honey. Who educates them. Who picks them from the mire and makes them ministers and generals. ...'

The conjure-woman was now using her ten-fingered wooden comb to straighten the hair.

'Oh Christ, Oh Christ. ...'

A deacon carrying a picture of one of the scenes of hell was now standing near the conjure-woman. The devils had tied down a naked man and were butchering him, the blood flowing from every part of the body, shown with dull yellow. At the right-hand section of the same picture, the remains of the unfortunate man were being pounded with mortar and pestle.

'Oh, yes, you should pay for it! You need only look at the picture to imagine what it would be like in hell, though I admit, what you see in the picture is very, very insignificant as compared to what awaits you. ...'

Another thin, crane-like deacon was carrying a picture of St George. He was shown mounted on a horse and proudly looking towards the direction of the preacher, while at the same time on his left killing the dragon by piercing it with his lance through the mouth. The dragon was in his death-throes, and a small ugly devil with short horns, very large sharp teeth, a tail and uncloven hoof, who had been using the dragon for a mount, was grovelling in the dust.

'Oh Christ, Oh Christ
'Oh Amlak, Oh Amlak. ...'

'And this is the beginning (pointing to the *tabot*) the beginning of the result of our crimes, of our sins. And all of us know what it means when our beloved Saint refuses to enter His tabernacle. Oh, yes, we all know! We all know what it means. It means bad harvest, locust, plague, hunger, death and devastation of men and animals alike ... the approach of Doomsday. ...'

'Oh Egzyo, Oh Egzyo
'Oh Egzyo, Oh Egzyo. ...'

She was now using her *degan* (a kind of bow) and her *kel-anget* (the neck of a gourd), and, singing her beautiful melody over his head, was gently picking at the sinew string in his hair with the edge of the *kel-anget* to lighten and straighten it, and give it the wispiness of a cirrus cloud.

'Have I said, the *tabot* has refused to enter its tabernacle? Oh no! that's fooling ourselves. We'd rather say that it has refused to go even as much as near its church. Cancelling as we did the lunch that used to be given in his honour. Yes, it has refused to move and all because we have forgotten our duties to our Church, our Emperor and our country ...' He waited to see the effect he was making, rearranged his attire of leopard skins on his shoulders, struck the ground with the staff he was carrying – a staff ornamented with a cross and rings of brass – and started to roar again louder than ever.

'Kerarayeso, Kerarayeso
'Oh Egzyo, Oh Egzyo. ...'

The chanters were doing their best, it seemed, to drown the roar of the preacher.

'We have sinned against our God, we've sinned against our Emperor, against our country, against our brothers, against society, against ourselves – and great, great indeed is the price we have to pay for all of these. . . .' The conjure-woman suddenly realized what she was doing. Her whole body trembled; her shoulders shook as if she were in a fit, and in a sort of stupor, deaf and blind to everything around her, she ran out of the crowd towards the *wanza* shade. A heron, her long neck outstretched, rose from the tree, flapped lazily across the face of the sun, sailed towards the grove of *koso* trees around the church, circled it two or three times, uttered a wild and piercing cry, and came back and landed where she had started.

The priest bearing the *tabot* on his head was carefully supported from falling down by two other priests, who during the procession shaded the *tabot* from the heat of the sun with multi-coloured umbrellas.

'Yes, my children, it's time for repentance. It's the time to save ourselves from everlasting hell-fire. Yes, my children. And let those who have sinned against their Emperor confess their crime and take their punishment – for it's written, it's better to lose the kingdom of this world than to lose the kingdom of heaven. Better it is to receive the punishment of an earthly king than that of God. And that it is better to suffer an earthly prison than the prison of hell where the devil's teeth are sharper than the sharpest cutter on earth. . . .'

'Oh Christ, Oh Christ
'Oh Christ, Oh Christ. . . .'

' . . . Where the worms and beasts know of no rest, no sleep but munching us without swallowing, subjecting us to everlasting torture. Oh, my children, how can a mortal like me conceive for you the punishment that is ahead? It's frightening. It's inconceivable. It's better indeed to pay for our sins in an earthly prison. . . .'

The priest was still fixed at the spot where he had stopped. The two priests were still holding him up. And it looked as if no amount of sing-song or preaching or penance would move him.

'Kerarayeso, Kerarayeso
'Oh Amlak, Oh Amlak. . . .'

'Even our everyday life – our everyday life is being affected and slowly destroyed by our sins and crimes. Our quiet and simplicity of home life has started to give way to violence and indifference. Our national character, faith, will-power, habits of reverence, of industry and devotion to duty, are dissolving in the mists of innumerable artificialities and fads which have claimed our entire personality – drinking, dancing, prostitution and the like. . . .'

'Kerarayeso, Kerarayeso
'Kerarayeso, Kerarayeso. . . .'

' . . . The marriage union has been cheapened. It's lightly entered into and lightly set aside. Our courts are congested with suits for divorce, and squabbles over land about the removal of landmarks, not paying the interest on grain loaned for sowing. Submission to authority has also declined. Parents' authority is ignored. . . .'

'Oh Christ, Oh Christ

'Oh Amlak, Oh Amlak. . . .'

' . . . Yes, my children – the Judgement Day has come. It shall reveal the secrets of all hearts with their purity or with their wickedness. And we shall very soon pass from death into life in Christ, or into eternal damnation in Satan. And that's the beginning' (looking towards the *tabot*) 'of the punishment. . . .' He looked at the conjure-woman who was in the way of his finger, and then at the *tabot* and at the conjure-woman again (gazing longer this time) and then at the *tabot* and sharply at the conjure-woman. The conjure-woman noticed, and sent her son to stand by his tree in acknowledgement. The preacher on his part noticed the gesture. 'Let those who have eyes see and those that have ears listen. We have sinned, it's true! But we still have our understanding. We know we can be re-born again fresh and law-abiding through Christ our Lord. . . .'

'Oh Amlak, Oh Amlak

'Oh Christ, Oh Christ. . . .'

'We can regain our beauty, our purity of heart, our freedom. The Lord God will by-pass our faults with his kindly and forgiving eyes. He is always ready to forgive us. If we only repent and take penance. Oh yes! He's always ready to receive us. To forgive us. But penance, we must take. . . .' He uttered the last words with energy, looking, it seemed, towards the conjure-woman.

The blurring shimmer of heat waves and the glare of the sunlight on the volcanic rocks around became more and more unbearable. And as she stood under the *wanza* and watched, it seemed to her as if everything was moving. The preacher went on louder and louder, the mules were still squealing and the sun quivering and flaming. The conjure-woman felt quickness of life engulfing her on all sides. She looked for the second time towards the preacher. He was still gesturing, gesticulating and talking. And it looked as if he was addressing her more and more. Her hands started to play with the pink kerchief – now covering her hair with it and now sliding it down her neck – faster and faster.

'Yes, Christ understands and forgives our weaknesses. . . . ' He looked at the conjure-woman and then at the *tabot*, 'After all, aren't we all his children? We are! And He knows that there are weeds in us. Wasn't that why Christ was sent to this world: to separate us from what chokes us in its midst and make us His own; gently to pull out the weeds that trouble us, that choke us and kill our beauty, with his delicate and loving hand? Oh yes, we are God's garden if only we would allow Christ to be woven into the fabric of our person. . . .' His words were meant to be mysterious and of multiple meanings. So that seeing the various interpretations, the rabble would stand in awe of everything uttered.

'Oh Christ, Oh Christ

'Oh Amlak, Oh Amlak. . . .' was still competing with the preacher from the other side.

'You are God's garden if only you would allow Christ to be woven into your everyday life – into your feelings – into your dreams and hopes. . . .' He looked at her again, this time his eyes staying on her without wavering, 'You are the chosen delicate tree full of sap and green that God has planted. And as true as I am on this tree, true it is the desire that suddenly rose in me to rest under your shadow. That may be why the Lord God has brought me to your view. . . .'

The conjure-woman watched the movement of his eyes, still playing with her kerchief. Her look grew more and more languid, and her eyes more and more playful. And suddenly a revelation – it occurred to her that she was, after all, all the while ready to take penance and regain her oneness with Christ. And in an outburst of agitated feeling, she trotted back to the preacher. And on the way, a thorn gave her foot a keen and sudden jerk.

'Oh Christ, Oh Christ

'Oh Amlak, Oh Amlak. . . .'

'That may be why He has subjected me to the will of the wind – to be blown to your side – to rise from the ground – to grow – to strengthen – to get broader and richer in my trunk and to protect you in all atmospheres and through all weathers. . . .'

'Oh Amlak, Oh Amlak. . . .'

The dancing heat waves were slowly beginning to give way to a general warmth. She felt something lifting her soul – her eyes opened – opened as if expecting something great – and she looked at the picture of Jesus Christ as for the first time. She couldn't again believe her eyes – that unmistakable resemblance between the preacher and Christ.

'Oh Amlak, Oh Amlak

'Oh Amlak, Oh Amlak. . . ,' the loud and prolonged chorus rose and fell.

'Oh, how many of us look for trees only on a hot day by the rocky, dusty roadside, and blind ourselves to their heavenly beauty. How many of us deaden the spiritual poetry they excite in the heart. The delicate and intricate flow of the human spirit. . . .'

'Oh Christ, Oh Christ

'Oh Amlak, Oh Amlak. . . .'

The chorus rose up to the high heavens, died away with the reverberating echoes from mountain to mountain – and rose again almost as quickly.

'I say to you again and again – submit yourself. Give your heart to Christ before it's too late. . . ,' his eyes widened and glittered. She listened in perplexity to the sounds which her dreamy imagination was conjuring up. She listened to the ever-louder chorus. All around her, people, animals and plants took on the guise of diaphanous shadows. And then something strange and joyous that almost brought tears to her eyes happened to her.

' . . . to Christ who will search you – who will inspect you how adequately or inadequately you are equipped . . .'

She was bemused by the heat and the pain of the thorn in her foot. Gradually, in her mind, the thorn became transferred into the preacher's. She looked at his bare feet – quite small as compared to his body. They looked to her unused to being bare. She felt the pain he was feeling – she went nearer to his feet to extract the thorn with her nipper.

A warm breeze mingled with the scent of *wanẓa*, jessamine and grass flowers, encircled the preacher. Hanging branches brushed his head. And from time to time they dropped a leaf or two on his shoulders, neck and lips. A whirlwind passed the trees, emerging from what seemed a dead calm. Myriads of undefined sensations quickened his heart. The shadow on the ground had become more agitated as if trying to rise and fly away – and the conjure-woman touched his foot.

' . . . to Christ who will cherish you – to Christ who will cleanse you and purify your heart – who will lighten your body – to Christ who will keep your heart forever in His light and splendour – to Christ. . . .' She touched his foot for the second time. 'To Christ who offers you' (meeting the fire in the eyes of the conjure-woman with the fire in his) 'the sacrament. . . .'

'Oh Christ, Oh Christ
'Oh Amlak, Oh Amlak. . . .'

' . . . Look at Christ . . . Look at Christ! And follow Him. And Him only. . . .' The conjure-woman was looking not at the picture he was pointing at, but at him – her eyes were wide open. 'Look at Christ! Get his definition of life. Let Him work on your heart and make you a living being of wholeness and happiness, for without Him, we are disembodied spirits who will accomplish nothing. . . .' The preacher was still speaking, but without fire, without feeling – dead. And suddenly, with regard to nothing new at all, he cried out like a man who, despairing of immediate assistance, has lost all hope; and shaking and beating himself on his forehead, made a show as if frantically struggling against something that was forcing him to pull his head from his shoulders. He jumped down from his tree and trotted up to the church.

And at long last, the *tabot* started to move.
Following him slowly upwards—
The brave-looking warriors
The horses and mules
And the rabble.

2 The Attainment

Goytom

The *tabot* bearer mounted the stairs that led to the big gate in the fence of the church with difficulty. And before he made his three rounds of the church to get in, he stopped by the main door trying to catch his breath, and listening to the reading of the Life of Abbo.

'. . . wearing the bark of trees for clothes, eating roots and leaves, living in the open and sleeping on the hard ground at night . . .' one of the priests read. The pilgrims were standing all over the yard, listening. He expatiated on Abbo's chastity, simplicity, innocence and holiness. He read about the taming of the devils of Zekwala. About how Abbo used to send lightning to subjugate them. About how he rode on lions and leopards. And how, once upon a time, he gave one of his eyes to a thirsty bird which happened to alight on his head.

The piquant little lady, standing near the *tabot*-bearer, was talking to the minister's wife. A woman with an enormous body, she looked like the strong *wanẓa* and fig planks of which the doors of the church were made. They are made with no hinges: the side frames are in one piece and fit into the holes in the lintel and floor plates. She was sway-backed to an amazing degree. Must have been lugging a big earthen jug on her back when she was young, or have been used to sitting long hours, to have developed such buttocks, protruding behind and upwards for the jug to rest upon. Or for the master. Such . . . such, such a shelf . . . a platform. And her arms like those two heavy bars of the door. Massive bulks of timber. And what a contrast to the little lady. Like the flat stones that give out a metallic sound. The thin flat stone. And the thick and bulky flat stone. Both hanging from a very old tree. And when struck by a piece of hard wood, the thin stone gives a low, clear tone, and the thick one, a deep, muffled sound. The stone bells of Abbo.

Musicians making a sentimental, plaintive sound upon their one-stringed instruments, led the way. The incense bearers, swinging their copper vessels with their dense white incense smoke, came next. Then, the *tabot* with all its retainers – priests, dignitaries, merchants and farmers. And all of them walked around the church three times.

And no sooner had the *tabot* entered the church than pande-monium broke loose. With knives and swords in their hands, men and women ran after flesh. And everywhere in the churchyard, they began to slice the sacrificial animals alive. One cutting – another snatching – one struggling – another running. Everywhere in the churchyard animals being carved up before they kicked off, one cutting from the hind leg, another from the foreleg, another from the stomach. And Abbo pleased at what was taking place. At least according to the belief of the people. Abbo pleased – left only with fragments of hides, refuse, and offal of dead animals. Abbo pleased – with offal and refuse and none of it buried. The hawks swooping down on the churchyard. Flies swarming and buzzing over a lump of meat. Pandemonium – the stench of spilt blood and incipient decay; the scene of damp grass; the cries of beggars; the barking and prowling of dogs. Everything about it – chaotic and primordial. . . . And then, the usual thunderstorm from out of nowhere. Commencing with a violent hailstorm, with hailstones as large as *wanza* nuts. And then turning into sleet rain. And then stopping just as suddenly as it had begun – the blazing sun.

I went down to the conjure-woman's hut to see how Fitawrary was doing.

Part Ten

1 The Little Lady

I said to my friend that if ever I get married, my husband is not going to be from the palace. I told her that he will be from a hermitage. Hidden away in the forests from prying eyes. I told her that I will be out soon looking for him. By some pool of water tucked away in the rocks, I will find him, I told her. A man of cheerfulness, restrained speech, helpfulness. . . .

And she said, 'You have to perform the appropriate sacrifices and rites before your guardian angel will lead you to him.'

And I told her that I shall spare no expense. That I have already allotted one bull each for Abbo and Saint Gabriel on their anniversaries.

'Why, I saw you breathe a long-drawn-out sigh when the sermon at the hill was concluded,' she said.

And how I lied to her. That the whole sermon was a piece of fluff. And that the preacher did nothing but wallow in a sense of self-satisfaction.

And she said, 'Your face clearly bore traces of excitement. And I was seized for you with a little pang. As if beaten by a guilty conscience.'

Again, how I told her that I was perhaps angry with the preacher for trying hard to practise deception upon the people. And for his working upon their superstitious gullibility.

'The tongues of false priests are coated with truth on top, like a lure for flies,' she started then.

'Didn't you notice his wan attempt to speak about God?' I asked her. Trying to support her argument. Not realizing at the time where it was leading me.

'A dolt can pass for a genius at such places as this,' she said, 'and as you may have noticed, some of the things he said tuck themselves in the memory like a half-forgotten laugh.'

How right she was. A half-forgotten laugh! That part about Christ being woven into our everyday life. Into our dreams and hopes. And that part about the chosen tree full of sap that God has planted. And the hope that we can regain our beauty, our purity of heart, our freedom . . . like a half-forgotten laugh! How right she is And those myriads of undefined sensations that rose up in me Strange and joyous sensations that brought tears to my eyes. And then I couldn't believe what I thought I heard her say.

'He was a waiting petitioner on my late husband's list for over a year.'

'A waiting petitioner?' I said. 'You mean to tell me that he is an ordinary mortal like you and me?'

'And before that he was a Captain in His Majesty's secret service branch. He was discharged from his service dishonourably for what he had said and done during the last *coup d'état.*'

I was so dumbfounded I couldn't utter a word. I couldn't even ask her about how he came to be a preacher.

But she went on, 'My late husband found him this job. You might say to help him expiate his past crimes on these lonely hills. And I suppose the authorities have already pardoned him. He has been very useful here as you may have noticed. And at the end of this year, perhaps, he may again be returned to his job.'

And what about the plaited and matted hair? I asked her. I was so dumbfounded. The plaited hair. The matted hair.

'It's all artificial. You must be quite ignorant of the world if you haven't noticed the delicacy of his bare feet. They do not look accustomed to being bare,' she said. 'Even my peasant and his conjure-woman can detect that much.'

'That's why his face looked younger to me,' I said, hiding all the other things that he looked like to me. It was foolish of me not to have avoided the subject of the sermon and the preacher. At least I shouldn't have allowed it to go that far. And what would she have said if I had told her about my spayed goat and about my bathing in the holy water with Captain preacher pouring the water through the silver cross and touching my body? What would she have said to that? Who knows? That disciple-attendant of his may be a corporal.

'The whole world is not an enormous injustice though, as the young men and women of today are pleased to stigmatize it,' she said. 'It's not a derision, it's not a mockery. It's not . . .' she said.

159

I waited to listen to what it was if not all that. . . . I waited and waited. But she didn't say it. She didn't tell me what it was. She simply mounted her mule and said good-bye to me and cantered homewards followed by all those handsome young retainers of hers.

I wonder what this world really is . . . if not that . . . that which one is anxious to have . . . that . . . a huge tree entwined by creepers – look at that stag-horn fern grasping the tree-trunks. Oh, my God! This mule is giving me a creepy feeling with her trick of going to the edge of the path and peering over the sloping sides . . . and with the small avalanche of small stones giving way under her foot. . . . This is the world, perhaps?

2 *Woynitu*

Goytom comes through the door with a lighted cigarette and a cloud of smoke wafting behind him. The hut is cold and the air has a sour stale odour – the mixed smells of wood, cow-chips and leather. The hostess is struggling to kindle a fire. She has broken sticks for kindling over her knee and arranges them on the foundation of cow-chips. At first the fire will not draw. The flames quiver weakly and are smothered by a black roll of smoke. The draught gives the fire new life. And the cowchips glow and the sticks catch fire, burning slowly – the shadow of the wavering light lapping against the walls . . .

Goytom sits on the raised earth of *medeb* in a corner like a man who is blind and dumb. Each muscle in his body looks rigid and strained. He seems to listen to something far far, away. Not caring to look around him. Isolated and angry and alone. Everything about him tense and sullen . . .

And I feel myself sinking downwards, slowly in wave-like motions, downwards in a shadowed hut. In helplessness, I strain my eyes, but I can see nothing except the dark and the waves of light that are roaring hungrily over the wood. And my father stretches his hand towards Goytom. And Goytom doesn't even see him. I go to him to see what he has in his hand. And he simply stretches it towards Goytom. I go and awaken Goytom from his reverie. He comes to his father.

'You keep this for me,' he says to him. Goytom takes it. It is a pocket watch. A big one, 'It has been with me for fifteen years now,' continues Father. 'And I never had to take it to a watch-maker,' he says. Goytom starts to examine it in the semi-darkness.

In a corner the peasant has been gulping his cabbage soup and is now wiping his mouth with the back of his hand.

'It is not an ordinary watch,' says my father.

'Yes, it's an Omega watch,' says Goytom.

'No, I don't mean that . . .' cuts in my father. 'It is a gift given me by our Emperor.'

'You must have done something extraordinary to merit this from him,' says Goytom.

'Oh, I was also raised in my rank and I was given land,' says my father, his voice going down to his throat.

'What am I supposed to do with it?' asks Goytom.

'You keep it for me! And use it . . .'

'But I have my wristwatch . . .' argues Goytom.

'No, that is for show, and this is for work!' says Father. 'And I want you to remember me with my good deeds as well,' he continues. I have never heard him talk that way before. And I feel as if I am losing him . . .

'Why do you stand there moping like that!' says Goytom irritably. I think he is feeling the way I feel and he is angry again. Perhaps with himself. Perhaps with me. He goes to his spot in the corner and sits looking at the watch. Looking at the hard beaten ground. And then, it seems, he can't sit still and he goes out . . . How I wish I could snuggle up to him and cry . . . But he goes out to be by himself – he goes out . . .

I go out too and sit down by myself on a dead log covered with wild moss under a tree – listening to my heart – listening to the wind in the canopy of leaves above.

3 The Conjure-
woman

Goytom

A strong wind raged through the night. A jackal howled near by.
The shadow of the soot-laden ceiling hung in the hut. As though it
would fall on us any time. The flame of the little wax candle
flickered. Blown this way and that by the wind. Seeking calm and
always likely to go out. And the sleepy eyes of the conjure-woman
assumed an air of stern activity. And we waited goggle-eyed for the
approach of the devils.

Now and then, the priest belched the undigested meat of our black
sheep. He poked me in the ribs. Slapped me on the back. Assured
me of Fitawrary's recovery, by invoking God on high, honour and
the ashes of his ancestors. Now and then, we saw Fitawrary stretching his arms to relieve the cramp in his elbows. We heard his hard
breathing. Trying to stifle the feeling of heaviness in his heart. At
one point, we saw the peasant trying to light the fire in the hut. The
hut got filled with smoke. It drove Woynitu and me out to the yard
for fresh air. Even the priest emerged rubbing his eyes. And when
we got back, the peasant had already tossed out the wet sticks and
added some dry ones instead. He was blowing at them. And we
waited goggle-eyed, waiting for the appearance of the devils. In the
form of men, perhaps. With tails no bigger than common spindles.
Or in the shape of black kittens. We didn't know yet. And God only
knew what they had in mind in consenting to visit us. They might
thrash us with pitch forks and chains. Grunting and floundering
about a bit, Fitawrary was patiently lying on his back and waiting.

Then we heard a cry. A sudden, piercing, mournful cry that
seemed to come from around the lake. Some minutes later, the same
cry was repeated. But farther off. The peasant went outside. As if
he wanted to check. And then, we heard other sounds. The howling
and screaming of a group of jackals. Maybe they had found a fallen

animal somewhere. And then fleas started to come out of the hollow stalks of the dried grass. And up they climbed finding their ways through our trousers. The priest added a pinch of incense on the three broken earthen pots. The conjure-woman stirred into activity. She gave vent to a series of mumbles, snorts and grunts. She gestured and spoke in some unknown language – at least not known to me. Now calling the devils by name. Now indulging in a series of frenetic quakings and contortions. And then, a shower of stone rained on the hut. Strange and unholy voices filled the air. I wanted to check what was the matter. I rose up. But the priest pulled me down in time. He said it was the sign of their coming. He called them the unnameables. The conjure-woman apropos of nothing at all shrieked and started beating herself with a staff. She howled like a jackal. Brayed like a donkey. Bleated like a goat. Fitawrary craned his head and pricked up his ears and started to look out of the hut. The priest told us to hold fast to the *qat* branch the conjure-woman had given us. And not to look up if we heard them approaching. Nor if we heard them provoking us with their pranks and antics, and indecent noises. Even if you heard them expel flatus while dancing, never look up, he said. They would blind your eyes and cripple your body. And we promised to do as we were told.

And then Fitawrary started to say something. Something like he was almost losing his patience with the unnameables. His voice though should have been harsh. But it wasn't. It wobbled and cracked. Then something glided by the door. The priest told us to hold fast to the *qat* branch, not to look up. And again something glided. Slowly this time. I couldn't help looking at it. I couldn't believe in the unnameables blinding me. Or crippling me. I saw that Fitawrary was working with his right hand under his pillow. He was also staring hard at the door. He didn't seem to believe that part of the story either. He stared and stared and stared. His eyes widened suddenly, as though they were popping out of his head. Again a glide. A shuffle. A deafening shot from my father's pistol! And a shriek of pain from outside.

'I've got my enemy!' cried out Fitawrary. He rose for a moment as if he had got all his energy back. 'At last!' he hissed. And fell back across his litter.

And then slowly, he tried to straighten himself up. He motioned me to his side. He tried to whisper something into the hollow of my ear. His face convulsed. His eyes opened wide. A rattling sound escaped from his throat. His voice was like the soughing of the wind in the leaves. And that expression that I saw at the church broke out over his face. And he hugged me on to his chest.

For the first time in my life, I realized that he was my father, after all. He even made me forget that he was a sick man and I was pressing him down with my weight. I started to rise. And as I was doing so, his arms slid from my back and fell limp by his side.

He was dead.

Part Eleven

1 The Preparation

Goytom

The conjure-woman had been in some deep turmoil and had fallen from her stool when the accident happened. And she was in a state of stupefaction until early in the morning. When she regained consciousness, however, she seemed to know what had taken place, and set to work immediately. With the help of the priest, she washed the dead body of her husband and laid him on his bedstead.

And the servants and I did the same: we washed my father, dressed him and laid him on the litter.

Then, some priests were called in to perform the usual funeral rites and incense-burning.

Late in the morning, the district chief came along and told us to wait until the police came from Bishoftu and checked the accident. And we stayed – waiting vigil by the dead bodies.

2 The Conjure-woman

By noon, I hope the police will have come and I will be able to perform the funeral dances and songs for my husband. And by then, my priest friend will have returned with the wood coffin from Bishoftu. At least, I will bury my man as never anybody has been buried before.

But now, sitting here and keeping vigil over the bodies, and going back over and over again on the things I had done till now, I wonder at what point I went wrong. And at what I have done to merit all this. Were they all in vain – the fastings, the incense burning, the offering of sacrifices, the exorcising of demons in the name of God – why should this be my reward?

I shouldn't perhaps have tolerated his eating the meat of the sacrificial animals. And I shouldn't have allowed him to be intimate with the unnameables. Painting himself black for them. Dancing for them. Heralding their coming. And bragging about his connections. But haven't I told him often times to keep it in confidence? Not to talk about them in public? And haven't I told him about his keeping his cleanliness? He may have done things he shouldn't have done with that wife of the clerk. For otherwise, she wouldn't have put that pat of butter on his head. And with that titillating *ades* scent in it! And with the white paper she wrapped his head in! It's possible she bewitched him and made him unclean. It is possible he forgot his role of the night. But then, the unnameables! Shouldn't they by-pass such a mistake for once? Hasn't he served them loyally? Wasn't it even with their permission that he used to partake of their meat? If it wasn't, why didn't they kill him the first time he did it?

Oh my God, help me to find out where I went wrong. To make amends for the past. And to be able to learn something for the future. Help me to make the unnameables respond to my calls tonight. I am going to do all the appropriate sacrifices and incense burning, and beg of them to tell me of the wrongs I have done to them, and of my role in the future. And if they don't answer me, it may mean that I am out of favour and no longer in their service – or it may mean the end of my life is at hand too. In that case I shall prepare a place for myself by my husband's side . . . take penance . . . take the sacrament . . . take . . .

3 *Woynitu*

. . Keeping vigil by these bodies, oh God, I feel as if I'm lost with them. For everything has gone black. And yet, I'm lost with You more. With You I know not even who You could have been. . . . How am I to know how to approach You and know You nd perhaps . . .

Part Twelve

1 The Delay

We waited for the police until nightfall. They didn't come. And then on the morrow, we waited for them. They didn't come. Already, the hut had begun to reek of cadaver – a fearful stench. We decided to start on our journey on the morrow. With or without the police.

2 The Descent

Goytom

The winding mountain of Zekwala. There it lay. Hills, hills and hills. Below those hills, more hills. And below them, more hills. And below them all, the flat grassy land full of grey mist. Mists which grew wider and wider as you went downwards towards them. Mists which ascended towards you. Enormous blocks of stone on your way. With often a depth of two to three feet between each step. Scarcely possible in many places to reach the bottom without a fall. And the dust rapidly churning and churning into mud from the night's rain. Herds flowing down from the hillocks churning it. The foals gambolling in the grey mist below churning it. Churning it into mud. Making it difficult to walk on. And the cold wind hissing on our faces. The litter swaying rhythmically. The fearful stench spreading. Growing stronger and stronger at every step. The vultures flying over us. Trying to alight on my father's body. A hungry jackal sallying forth to attack us unawares. The sun coming out in intensity from behind the clouds. And hiding back again. Pedestrians holding their noses with their fingers and running away. A native in one of the hillocks whinnying like a tired horse

Crooning loudly one of those protracted ditties. Joined by another in another hillock. And then the two voices. Floating upwards, one following the other. From hill to hill. From mountain to mountain. Becoming stronger and stronger. Seeming to amplify our misery. Amplifying the despondency that already strangles us. Wailing up! Wailing up! The song. The smell. Stirring within our numbed heart. Revealing gnawing heart-ache. Reopening old wounds. Waking to anguish. And then the stop. One of the singers stopped to listen to the singing of the other. The same wailing, weeping, and stirring. And the start. He started again to blend his voice once more with the common billow of sound. Swelling forth like a wave. A dense wave of sounds. Presenting itself to the mind as a road. A road stretching far – far – far away. A broad road under an unpredictable sun. A scorching sun. A clouded sun. With us walking along the enormous blocks of stone. With two or three feet between each step. Scarcely possible to reach the next step without falling. And the cloud-pushing wind blowing. Our eyes reddening with exposure to it. Our faces blackening with dust and sweat. The protracted ditties continuing. Whinnying like a tired horse. A sadly caressing motif, perhaps. Lightening the heaviness of the singers' soul. Whinnying like a tired horse. The ringing neigh of a steed answering a mare from one of the hills. Woynitu vomiting. And I trying to help. Not much of a help. I started to vomit too. Vomitsng out my intestines or my liver or something like that. Shaking as if with fever. And then our servants brought down my father's litter under a tree. They walked farther off to another tree and started arguing. Woynitu and I vomiting. And then the cry of the old woman – a passer-by. A vulture! A vulture was sitting on my father's head, plucking at his face. She tried to chase him. But even the vulture seemed to realize that she was only an old woman. One of the servants chased him away. Tears welled up in the woman's dim, small eyes, merging with the wrinkles on her grief-stained cheeks. And then the news. One of the servants refused to carry the body any farther. I couldn't force him to do it. I started carrying it myself along with the other three. The smell came stronger and stronger. The sun went on playing hide-and-seek. I stopped. I realized, by the way I was feeling, that I wasn't strong enough to make the journey of over one hundred and sixty kilometres on foot.

I said to the servant who refused to carry the litter, I will pay you fifty dollars. He came to my rescue. And then, another one refused. I told him that I would pay him the same fifty dollars. He refused. One hundred dollars. He refused. One hundred and fifty. He refused. Two hundred dollars. He agreed. Then the last two brought down the litter at the same time. A lot of bickering followed. They agreed on three hundred and four hundred and fifty dollars each. . . .

And then we heard an unexpected thunderstorm somewhere near by. Followed by a shower of rain. And innumerable hail-stones. Slapping our faces. Drumming on the body of my father. Drumming on Woynitu. Drumming on me. Making spring-boards of us all. On the rebound. And we too were drumming on Zekwala – on the rebound. And yet like the Ethiopians we were, slowly and respectfully we trudged down. Respectful of the deceased. Respectful of the thorn-covered bushes and paths. Respectful of the churned and muddy road ahead of us.

And then the stopping of the rain just as unexpectedly. The momentary fading away of the bad smell. And the moment's silence.

In the distance, the morning train to Dire-Dawa. Rumbling and roaring and emitting vigorous chuffs of steam. Attaining pitch and tone. Wending its way down following the telegraph poles. Following the electric poles. Following the bill-boards: 'Smoke Nyala' 'Smoke Elleni', 'Smoke Axum – Filter American Blend', 'Fly Ethiopian Airlines– thirteen months of sunshine . . .'

Glossary of Amharic Words

Abujedid – muslim.

Ades – powder with fine scent made from the leaves of the 'ades' plant.

Agafari – an usher and door-keeper.

Angetlebse – a small cotton outer garment for children.

Begena – an eight- or twelve-string musical instrument.

Bernos – a black woollen cape.

Besanna – an evergreen tree, cultivated chiefly for its wood used in ornamental work.

Das – a temporary shelter made of a framework of stakes, and covered with leaves, goat, and sheep-skins.

Debteras – churchman (title).

Emboi – the fruit of a thorny shrub.

Erbo – utensil used to measure a quantity of cereal (smaller than a *kunna*).

Ferenj – foreigner (European or American).

Fitawrary – title of a dignitary.

Ferazmach, Kegnazmach, Dejazmach – title of dignitaries.

Endod – the flowers of a tree used instead of soap by the peasants for washing clothes.

Injera – staple food among Ethiopians, a kind of large pancake.

Jiraff – a whip with a long lash of cowhide.

Katikala – Ethiopian equivalent of gin or vodka.

Kerar – a six-string musical instrument.

Kerare – thin drink made from the residue of the beer dough.

Koso – a tree cultivated for its flowers which are used as an antidote for tapeworm.

Kunna – utensil used to measure a quantity of cereal.

Netela – a light *shemma*.

Masinqo – a one-string musical instrument.

Medeb – earthen couch or bed.

Qat – narcotic plant, usually eaten by Mohammedans.

Ras – a title of a high dignitary.

Sefed – a tray-like kitchen utensil made of grass.

Sellecha – a goat-skin used as a grain container.

Shemma – toga-like outer garment traditionally worn by Ethiopians.

Tabot – the square canopy of the holy ark with the Ten Commandments.

Teff – Ethiopian cereal grain.

Tej – mead made of honey.

Tella – Ethiopian beer.

Teskar – a memorial feast given on the fortieth day after the death of a person.

Tukul – thatched hut.

Wancha – drinking utensil made of horn.

Wanza – an evergreen tree cultivated for its fruit and wood.

Washint – a musical wind-instrument similar to the flute.

Wot – curry-type sauce.

Woiba – an evergreen tree cultivated chiefly for its hard wood and for its flowers used to dye ecclesiastical garments yellow.

Wudemma – threshing floor.

Zelzel – a lump of meat cut into many chain-like pieces.